Turnipseed the Tooth Faerie

Jerry Kidd

Copyright Page

Turnipseed the Tooth Fairy

This is a work of fiction. Names, characters, places and incidents are either the product of the author's imagination or are used fictitiously, and any resemblance to actual persons, living or dead, business establishments, events or locales is entirely coincidental.

Library of Congress Control Number 2015913121

Published in Salt Lake City, UT.

Copyright 2011 by Jerry J.Kidd

ISBN-13:978-1475074673

ISBN-10: 1475074670

This book is dedicated to people like me who still like to go to the Forest Preserves like Orland Park Forest preserve near Chicago and wait for King Lars to come sit with them on a park bench, especially a favorite bench in the wooded area just overlooking the meadow. And if you're especially observant you'll get the unforgettable soft scent of apples and cinnamon and walnuts.

Chapter 1

Brimble is missing!

As every child knows, the night is left to the little creatures, who dare not show during the day. For it is not enough that daylight robs them of their consciousness, but also, during the day, their enemies of night, the spiders and lizards and oft times the cats, fear them not. At night, though, through some marvelous things we do not yet understand, the spiders and snakes and lizards cannot see or smell them. I suppose if they could, night time would be terrifying to the little creatures. But as daylight comes, with their little spells, they retire in safety, to their faerie homes.

Which is why, on this end of a moonlit night, for there was the most beautiful of all harvest moons, as Turnipseed lay upon her bed with a good mystery book trying to find Morpheus, she was aroused by a knocking at her door. She had the most marvelous of doors, as was befitting her station, for it was made of solid oak and hung from two beautifully scrolled hammered hinges that attached firmly in-letted into the wood. At the top, the door was rounded, and fit heavily into its' deep recess of her treebourne cottage.

"Turnipseed!" The voice was that of King Larseous, the king of all the little people. Well, king he was in name, but mostly the little creatures ruled themselves quite wisely without much help, thank you much. But in name and respect, he surely was. Not short, not stout, but vigorous and young, with shining dark auburn hair that he gathered in back, and tied in a tail with a deep red ribbon.

Turnipseed took her nightdress, spun of the finest of spider's silk, gossamer and dainty, somehow revealing, somehow not, and wrapping it around her made her way to the door and opened it wide.

She flipped on the outside light as she looked at the group. It was impressive -- the elite of the little creatures.

The king, without waiting for an invitation, barged past her into her drawing room, as kings are wont to do, and sat down heavily, as best a muscular person can do heavily, on one of the two sofa's. The others, not being kingly, politely stayed on the front porch.

I suppose there is a reason that you have invaded my privacy this early morning!" She sounded rather put upon, as she should certainly have sounded.

"You didn't see it on the telly this morning? And he paused. He was so used to watching the Big People's news he had subconsciously assumed that somehow the news he brought was important enough to have made the early news. "Such a foolish assumption," he thought.

"See what, Lars? There isn't much on the telly worth staying up late morning for, you realize! What a dreadful item, anyway! Talk, talk, talk! And all that trash in the morning. Well, you know, you judge the people moronic enough to watch, and not the show. It's only there because there are those who think it normal."

Really, the king thought, I hate it when she makes these side trips in reason. It's hard to believe that she's of such importance. And with that, he shut up his thinking. Because, he was not sure, anyway, if Turnipseed could read thoughts. For after all, her father did.

"No."

"No what, Turnipseed. "

"I don't read thoughts. I can, you know, and I did then, because after all, you aren't very gifted in keeping them to yourself."

"Bother!"

"Anyway, I'm not offended. I do go on about things, trifle things to you, I imagine. But I know I can be eccentric. It is a pity, though, about those terribly sick talk shows on the telly."

"No. You need to hear me out, Turnipseed, and forget the daytime telly, if you will. This is important -- for we have a crisis on our hands..."

"How lovely! A crisis! You don't say!" She furrowed her brow and stared intently at the king. "I'm not getting anything from you, dear. You're holding back on me!"

"I'm not holding back on you, " he said. "I'm so anxious, I'm not certain I have cognizant thoughts. You see...Brimble did not come back last night." It was said almost matter-of-factly, but in spite of the calmness in which he spoke, it portended a great possible tragedy.

It was serious. So serious, Turnipseed did not even continue attempting to read the king's thoughts, but indeed, cradled her head into her hand, her other hand supporting that elbow.

"Didn't come home, you say? And why not?"

"We don't know. Skinny Kenneth and Brimble were stopped to talk with the Field Mouse sergeant in arms in Fairbucket Meadow last night, and everything was normal. While he spoke to the Sergeant, why Skinny Kenneth went into Mouse's burrow for a thing or two to eat, and when he came back both the Sergeant and Brimble were gone. Evaporated, as it were, into nothing... Gone!" And finally his voice rose in concern. "If he's out more than several hours, not only will his power be drained, Turnipseed. But daylight, pure sunlight can sometimes kill leprechauns."

"Yes, yes! I do understand about leprechauns. It's because they are so Irish, so transparent of complexion, that the least amount of direct sun will cause him to burn and blister. You don't suspect that it was a cat or snake, do you," Turnipseed asked, now fully engrossed in the conversation, so much so, she had turned off her thought-captures so her mind could narrow in on the problem at hand..

"Not at all, Turnipseed, after all, how could they? It was still dark!"

"Yes, yes. I know that, Lars."

Now, kittens are fun and soft and cuddly to all little children the world over, but to the little people, they are as ferocious as the most fearsome Serengeti Lion. That is why, when Fairies and Elves began to roam the world, they were permitted by a Gracious One with the power of invisibility to all predators and enemies of the night. But daylight destroyed not only their magic to be invisible but all of their magic unless they were underground in their safe homesteads or in their tree bungalow like Turnipseed's own home where it was still black as night during daylight.

Turnipseed was different, for her power of flight and invisibility were assured for daytime as well as nighttime. As with all gifts, there were oddities -- glitches that still made venturing outdoors -- well, difficult.

For one thing, in the daytime, all creatures could smell her. And her scent was a delightful fruity mixture of raisins and nuts and all manner of other succulent fruits -- especially watermelons. Cats and snakes, obviously are not interested in fruit smells. But, ah, the danger came from overly friendly squirrels-- not being nocturnal animals-- who did not recognize the scent as that of Turnipseed, which obviously, all the friendly animals of the night did. When she was about in the day, the squirrels would sniff about and search everywhere, running up and down the tree, chattering quickly and loudly, as only squirrels do.

Lars was not one to stay seated long, he jumped to his feet and began to pace inside Turnipseed's small drawing room. His usual stance was to bend slightly forward, and then lowering his head, stare intently at the ground while he paced. Depending upon his mood he would pace in a circle if he were quietly contemplative. And if he were determined for a quick result, he would then stride off in one direction or another, and turn abruptly and walk back to the vicinity of his departure.

If he were truly vexed and knew not if he had an answer or just a hunch, he might circle for awhile, the stride going purposely here or there, or both! And since Turnipseed's small home could no longer control his space, it was necessary he step outdoors and purposely stride to the point where he could then go into his circle! He was King, of course, though not everyone followed every little thing he would do, out of respect to him, they did that night.

He motioned with his arm for Turnipseed to follow along. And she would have it no other way!

He would walk swiftly, leaving Turnipseed and the other's scarce with any breath at all.   And other times, he would abruptly stop as he would receive a brilliant idea. And then, again grasping his arms behind his back, bending slightly at the waist, would lower his eyes and stride again. As he did, there was a whir of small wings, and a dainty faery lightly touched her toe to the ground next to the king and softly settled to the ground, her wings still moving slowly through the air. She fairly burst with the telling of the news that she was bore.

It was all coming too fast for Turnipseed. When she tried to exclude the others and concentrate on the fairy's thoughts, it was a jumble of the king and the dragonflies thoughts mixed with those of the fairy.

All this was in the twinkling of a stardust speck. "Stop it, stop it!" she yelled, fairly clapping her hands over her ears, as if that would stop the cacophony of their thoughts. "One at a time! Pamela Morningstar (for that was the faerie's name, a know-it-all who had to be first to tell anybody what had happened, good or bad) Speak up, girl! You're all thinking at once, and I don't have a clue what she's going to say because it's just a great big babble!" she finished, addressing the others.

Fairies, as any child knows, are from the English Country side. And Ireland is the origin of the leprechauns and elves. There were some German elves present, but they mainly had intermarried with the English fairies, and oh bother! It was enough to make the head swim.   Especially since Turnipseed had to translate quickly from the Celt and German to proper American.

"Sergeant Mouse is home now, "Morningstar (fairies hate having their first names said aloud, superstition, you know) said in one short breath. But Brimble is not with him. In fact, he says he has no recollection of any of the nights events other than he found himself wandering about in the cattails and his head hurt terribly!"

The king and all his subjects immediately broke into a circle, and with an absurd air of authority, the king began to move in another ring about the clearing they had just entered. The king, holding one hand with the other behind his back reminded one more of an unrobed Cambridge lecturer than an honest to goodness faerie king. And with his head lowered to gaze into the grass, he led the procession. Out of respect, Turnipseed joined the tramping about. Everyone was talking out loud, which destroys all intelligent thought, anyway, and Turnipseed could see no use trying to thought tune anyone in, for their babble made their thoughts pure drivel.

It was an absurd looking ring, for there were all kinds of figures present. The king, rather ordinary -- one might mistake him for a one-foot high mortal -- and a strange band of rather knobby jointed dwarves and elves, Turnipseed in all her beauty, and now the Sergeant Mouse had made his way to the group and was tramping at the end of the line in the circle.

Presently the king, not looking so much where he was going as where he had been, bumped into the back of the Mouse Sergeant. It rather surprised the King, for he thought that the Mouse Sergeant must surely be in the safety of his burrow-home by now.

The king stopped short in surprise and as in reverse dominos, all those behind quickly stacked behind him.

"Sergeant", yelled out the King. "I am wanting to talk to you and you are running away from me!"

"Sorry, your Highness. I am trying to keep up with the expedition and I must hurry or I'll surely be left behind!"

"Sergeant -- don't' be an idiot! Soon enough you will find that they are following me...we're in a thinking circle, not an expedition!"

"That can't be, sir. You, after all, and I digress here, are certainly following me. Therefore, how in thunder can I be following you?" And at that, he hit the whole group, all coming to a standstill stacked against the king.

Turnipseed quickly tuned in the King and the king, shrugging, said: "And this, unfortunately, is the epitome of my kingdom!"

Turnipseed injected her voice into the King's head, "On the truest level, sir, the mouse is not actually a faerie, but an enchanted animal. Whether he is "of" your kingdom is certainly debatable."

And with that, she picked up the king again: "Turnipseed -- must you eavesdrop on everything I say? Can I have no privacy?" And with that, his mouth took over, and it was all babble, babble again, thought wise for incoming thoughts to Turnipseed.

The group, still wanting to tramp the circle, even without the king and Turnipseed and the Sergeant, began to tromp again, leaving their little sub-group heretofore mentioned in the center. But all faeries and little people are objectionably curious, and so the circle expedition or thought circle or whatever it is they are wont to call it, slowly stopped walking, and crowded around the threesome at the center.

"Your highness, I no longer had got home -- and late it was for some reason, and my wife told me that you had an expedition. Now I truly doubted that, being it was daylight and all, but then daylight never hurt any of my kind, you understand, sir. Because we have no magical powers you can think of other than the enchantments done to us. And great enchantments they are, too sir. For I jolly well like standing upright, talking and enjoying the telly and living for two hundred years, which I certainly would never have done had you not enchanted me long ago, sir! But I digress! I know it must be awfully so important as to have you sergeants and elves larking about during broad daylight when so much harm can come to you."

"If you keep up this digressing, disagreeable conversation much longer, it shall be dark, Sergeant! And there won't be any harm for us." He stopped and took a very kingly pose. "I am glad you did come, Sergeant. For Brimble is lost, and you were the last one to see him last night."

"I was? I don't remember -- I saw him, of course. We always see each other at the Pub where we have a little refreshment for our break. That's odd...I do remember him there...but I cannot tell you anything more than that..."

The king placed his hands on the epaulette shoulder of the Sergeant and look directly into the mouse's black eyes. "Think, rodent! Think! What can you tell us about your meeting? Anything at all, we are grasping!"

"I can't remember except that, sir! .... There was Brimble...I remember a couple of mouses" (mice really don't call themselves collectively 'mice' because it seems so belittling to them. After all, 'mouse' has one more letter than 'mice', so in polite societies, they always refer to each other as mouses. Of course, when they're alone, they use all types of mouse cussing, which we will keep from polite society as yourselves).

Turnipseed was the first to interject. "Sergeant, I keep hearing other thoughts -- almost like other voices rumbling around in your mind...can you hear them?"

"I needs to sit down, I am certainly tired, I got home so late," and with that, he used his spear as a pole to let himself gently to the ground, where he took off his floppy hat and wiping his forehead with his arm to wipe of the sweat, he turned to Turnipseed. "By golly you're right, your loveliness, I can hear others in my mind's ear, all right." And with that, he turned into his mind, and listened with such intent that everything else was oblivious to him.

Turnipseed spoke to him so all of the assembled group could hear her. "I'm in there with you, Sergeant!"

We all have stood in a cave and yelled and had our voices zing around the cave for several minutes. "Jerry ...Jerry ...Jerry...JERRY," and we are not certain if there is someone in the cave yelling back to us. That is how the Sergeants mind worked. There were all kinds of voices, as if the mice's brain was so empty, that all voices he had ever heard were still bouncing around in there. Turnipseed, however, was certain there was no one else in the Sergeants' mind. (For after all, how much can one mouse's mind hold? I am not certain I have ever discovered that, even though I have had many conversations with them -- not the plain field mice, but with the royal white mice, of course. Even they, however, have far less intelligence than others attribute to them.)

The king was very thoughtful..."You say that you met them at the pub...which is quite unlike what Skinny Kenneth has told us..

"Really?" The mouse Sergeant seemed genuinely perplexed by this last bit of information. "What did Skinny Kenneth have to say?"

"Why don't you tell us what else might have happened, Sergeant? He said you met at the meadow and he had a bite to eat at your burrow!"

That's right...we had drinks at the pub, but I do believe that Skinny is correct. We did meet in Fairbucket Meadow tonight...last night...whenever. I know that there was Skinny and Brimble -- seems to me someone else was there...I do remember more, now...!" And doffing his fancy Sergeant's hat, he scratched his head to show everyone he was starting to put the voices in his mind together. " I remember Skinny wanted to get a bite to eat, and I told him I had cold roast beef in the cooler in my home...I believe he went there...But Brimble and I. I don't believe we waited, we both wanted a bitter at the pub..."

"Go on, "Turnipseed prodded, and squatted down by him, taking his grey, gnarly little hand in hers. "Can you think who those other voices are? I heard them -- but second hand and all, I can't tell who they belong to."

"I can tell you one who ties in -- I believe Lodi and her Frog were there."

There was a stunned silence among all.

Then Turnipseed responded, standing upright again, tall and regal. "I do believe you're right. Now that you say the name, I can hear her in that voice, Sergeant. Yes indeed I can. And I do hear Addie Frog there, too! Oh, my, such a funny little croak he has to his voice, yes indeed." And Turnipseed smiled at her cleverness, to be able to hear the tones and nuances second hand clearly enough to identify Addie Frog from them. "But really, all that certainly is not grave enough to think that it has anything to do with Brimble's disappearance, now does it? Really, does it?" Superior people, or those who feel they are, seem to always ask the question twice, as if by their extreme intelligence they already have the answer and want to reinforce that answer by the repetition of the question upon their lesser listeners.

"I don't know one way or 'nother -- being that I had no idea in the first place that Brimble was even missing..." He shuddered with his next thought. "I hope the Snake's or cats don't have him. It's daylight still, after all. And he could be anywhere. Even dead."

The king turned to Turnipseed. "Do you see we need your help? I can't send anyone else into the daylight where they are going to be at the same risk as Brimble, Turnipseed. We need your help.

Turnipseed, the great and gracious faerie she is, did not need to be coaxed. For each faerie was part of the greatness of faeryland, and would leave a hole in the fabric of the magical world if even one of the most common elves were to be snatched away forever. She turned to the King. "Lars, I shall certainly help, of course I will. Because I can, I will. And Because I Will, I can. But I certainly can do neither standing here in my night clothes."

The king glanced toward her, where she stood against the light, and saw her delicate and beautiful outline through the gossamer. "You certainly should, Turnipseed. I see why!"

And with that, Turnipseed blushed, and flew back to her home. "My, my, my," she said, putting her finger against her check, which felt all warm still from the blush. She glanced around and saw the group standing , watching. "I shall contact you by thought shortly, Lars." And then flew on.

Chapter 2

Turnipseed Prepares

As her slippered feet touched the hearth of her door, she was still saying, "My, my, my" over and over again. Really, Turnipseed and the King had never been close. After all, she had oh so many children to see each night -- and while time would stand still for her (or else, really how could she ever see all the children she must at night.) to attend to her children bringing them shiny new coins in all the world's currencies, the king could only operate in real time. He would oversee his subjects, hold court, teach the younger elves the intricacies of magic and place enchantments on animals and so forth. While Turnipseed would often return to her home exhausted from compressing all that time into one night, the king would still be ready to attend parties and masked balls, all that go with being kingly.

Truly, Turnipseed was at the epitome of faeriedom and was truly not just the Tooth Fairy, but a bona fide faery queen! Being pragmatic and not a little bit exasperated at the hierarchy of magicdom, she was never much interested in anything but doing her duty to the children of the world and keeping her little home spotless and spit-clean. Certainly she had never had time for anyone to be remotely interested in her.

And so, on this fair faery day, she kept repeating, "Oh my, my." and feeling her cheeks once again heat with the kiss of a blush.

Enough of that. I am telling you about Brimble.

This is why Brimble is so important to the magic world. We all laugh at the thought of the rainbow and at its' end, the pot of gold. Well, it was true, sort of.

Brimble and Skinny Kenny were leprechauns, absolutely. They had immigrated to the United States at the request of the faerie king because after Sutter's Mill and the California gold rush, the faery king could see that gold would be important for the elves and the faeries. There were things that the little people could not provide themselves. After all, in the old world, they would dress in gossamer from spiders webs -- like Turnipseed still did-- but truly, most of them wanted the things that they saw the Big People have. Like clothes of wools and cottons and silks, and things like Televisions and radios and the like. And certainly, elves and faeries and the likes would never dream of stealing from the Big People. But with a gold coin, magically placed where a television had been, or a radio or beautiful clothes, it was more than a fair trade, you see. And certainly a barrel of brew was important for the English and Irish elves, and for the German magic little folk, it was a necessity!

So, the king and his little folk would camp along the river with the miners (who of course never saw the little folk!) and by night, they would go to the creeks edge, and there in the moonlight, the gold would practically call them, for it would lay sparkling and shining yellow in the sides of the creeks, and by the rocks and other places. They would gather it into big burlap bags as big as an elf itself and putting them into little carts, the faeries would fly them to the bank at night and trade the gold for coins in the vault. No banker ever complained, for the gold left them would far out-value the gold coins that were exchanged.

All the gold coins traded by those thousands of faeries those warm nights were put in a great fireplace kettle that had been blackened by two hundred years of use by then, every since it had come over on the Mayflower (that's also the very ship that the first English faeries came over on to find some fresh meadows and woods to roam and raise faery families. England just wasn't big enough for the thousands of faeries that lived then). And that fireplace kettle was placed for safekeeping where the Big People could not find it, though they read about it and yearned for it. How the Big People ever heard about it, no one knows to this day.

And as in the Old Country, the safest place to keep the pot is at the end of the rainbow. Because, no one ever has found the end of the rainbow. It's there, and you can find it. But not where the Big People looked. For they would scurry, trying to find the end of the rainbow during the day! Not knowing that rainbows always extend into the night. For the full moon gives a faery rainbow, surely it does. As beautiful, if not more so, than any that have graced the heavens when the sun bursts through after the rain has begun to quiet. For the faint light of the moon, reflecting the sun as it does, gives a delicacy to the night's rainbows that are broken by things as fragile as the fluttering of a butterfly's wings and flee quickly into the night. It's there -- at the end of that rainbow that the elves guard their gold. And the magic of the Night's Rainbow only opens into the night, which suits the elves and faeries just right, for that is when they have been given the gifts that allow them to live a long and merry life!

There are only few creatures who are privy to the elves and faeries -- and most of them are unlovable creatures such as toads, and sadly for they too are unlovable -- the mice. You see, as you saw by the sergeant, mice can really be wonderful fellows. Their hearts are big and their nature is loving. Their families are big and kind to each other. Whenever the faeries needed creatures of the Big World to help them, they would always go to the mice first, to enchant them. Enchantments of this sort are the most wondrous enchantments of all, for the result is always fortuitous and noble. Somehow, the joints of the mice change, and they rear up, upon their rear legs, which thicken and become muscular and capable of supporting the mice upon their legs. Their front legs easily transform into arms with fingers and proper fingernails. Even their faces change and become less mouse-like and more like yours and mine.

They acquire the full cranial capacity that allows them to speak and think as we do! They become almost like little people with all the capacities to love and have little babies that suckle on bottles and use diapers! They dress in wonderful clothes knitted and woven out of the finest fibers of angora and long cotton shreds. They dye them with brilliant yellows from dandelions and reds from the crushed petals of roses. Their browns are from the crushed shells of fall acorns.

Oh, and their little burrows are so cozy and redesigned with carpets woven of the down of robins and the soft kopeck from the heads of the fall cattails. The walls are smooth and pasted with the loveliest of wall paper patterns printed with dandelion sap on papers made from the pounded summer reeds of the cattail plants. The furniture which used to all be handmade for the little mice, normally are the finest chairs and amours bought from the toy shops made for dollhouses. And as always, gold and dollars always replace the furniture to the exact penny, including sales tax of course, for the faeries exchange the dollars as they are the ones who provide the mice with such beautiful accoutrements. On a soft summer eve, with the warmth of the day have come the sudden showers and the flashing thunders, the little families settle into their bungalows and listen to the patter of the rain outside while they drink their cups of catnip tea or their honey-sweet chocolate. Occasionally, there are knocks at the door and a faery or two will be extended an invitation to join their repast as they drink their chocolates and laugh and tell stories about when they were all little.

Their larders are always full, for mice are ambitious and hard workers at whatever they do -- whether they are mice as mice, or enchanted mice. The enchanted mice have all types of cold meats and natural foods, such as seeds of the wild geranium plants, which, we are told, taste as melons do, yet are firm enough to store for months at a time. They keep a whole root cellar of tubers from curly dock, and small potatoes and turnips. And in the deepest part of their homes, where it is always the coolest, are wheels of cheeses that the families have made. After all, one must always remember that one is, after all, a mouse, enchanted though that may be. The cheeses are exquisite Gouda and satisfying English cheddars and Swiss cheeses.

To repeat, their only enemies are daytime snakes and cats of all sorts. But at night, as was explained, the mice as well as the faeries themselves, they are invisible and unsmellable to all other non-faeries and non-enchanted creatures. Even the devious pit vipers who search by heat have all their senses destroyed regarding these creatures at night. No matter how hard the cat tries to see them in the dark, these predators never will be able to find these creatures because of the wonderful protections given to them.

The thing that Turnipseed most loved about the enchanted animals was their great love for all creatures, large or small. That is not at all what you would expect. For their little homes were so full of love of family and love of all creature-kind. Which she knew was precisely why the Sergeant had shown up for the meeting, even though it meant that he had to be about in the daytime, when his worst enemies had all their faculties to know that he was there. So dangerous as it was, she knew that in his little mouse heart was a huge concern for his friend Brimble and his honest desire to help find the missing Leprechaun.

Chapter 3

Ready for Anything!

The king was impatiently stomping about still, but now all of the creatures had realized that it was a kingly pouty-pout and not some new tromp through the meadows. They had all seated themselves amongst the toadstools and grass stems. There was some safety by being in a crowd and after all, how often did they get to enjoy the warmth of the late spring day, glorious as it was with bright sunshine, a wafting wind with the most delicate smells of flowers and freshly growing gardens with peas and carrots. Some even took out little clay pipes and stuffed them with the Indian tobacco seeds and leaves and laying upon the ground, let curly wisps of white float into the air.

Others, being the smarter, complained to them of the stench, and with the kings stern looks of warning to the offenders, soon the clay pipes were hidden away, and they cleared their throats and said "Rather" a lot and tried to downplay the whole situation.

"Barty!" It was a come-hither call from the tooth faerie. "Barty!"

Bartholomew is a strange name for a Yorkshire pig that stands a solid 8" high and is as pleasantly round as you wish. He lay in front of the fireplace which of course sat unlit in the late spring. In the morning, when he returned from the voyage with Turnipseed, he would sometimes stoke a fire and lay on the rug in front of the crackling little fire and close his eyes and dream that he were in the largest mud bath in creation, and would wallow about and snort like pigs do when they dream of such things.

At this moment, he was indeed involved in similar mental revels that Turnipseed hated to rouse him. But it was necessary.

"Barty?" Now it was coaxing and bidding in the tone.

"Must you wake me, Turnipseed? I was having the best of dreams. You know how you always remember them best when they are closest to your waking mind? I was in Hawaii -- on the north beach surfing. And the most beautiful wahine was sharing my board. Now I'll never know how it turned out."

"A true pity, I'm sure. But I do assume that she will be waiting for you in Morpheus when you return, my fat friend!" As with any strong woman, Turnipseed allowed no idleness or dawdling. There would be time enough later, but now! It called for action.

"I need your services now, my dear. It cannot wait until ev'ning. We must be off, for there is evil afoot!"

"Really? Evil?"

"I hope not dreadful evil. But I fear some is mucking about -- you see Brimble did not return last night!"

Barty was fully up, sitting back on his hind quarters, his mind was slowly awakening.

"Is the gold all there?" he asked. He knew the calamity if the little people were to lose their golden savings.

"We don't know, that is why we have to go see. It's you and I must find out, for we are the only ones who keep our powers during the day--" She was now dressed in her riding breeches and had a sheer silken blouse of purest white with a faint hint of pink that she loved so much.   She turned to the pig. "Quickly now, splash some water on your face, Barty. The king and the others are waiting in the meadow. We must find Brimble. Turnipseed and Barty came in together, but separate. Turnipseed was prone to let Barty carry her on her rounds, for they were very long, and Barty, being five times or so heavier than Turnipseed, had the stamina and power to go for hours upon hours without tiring his wings. Turnipseed, on the other hand, was less inclined to use her energy up on flying, when she could very well be whipped about on Barty's back, and all in the time it has taken you to read this paragraph he could be around the world at least once and still be from Chicago to Schenectady further along in the time it has taken you to read the last ten words. He was able to accomplish a great deal with Turnipseed. Or vice versa!

Barty was the first to notice below. "Where are they, Turnipseed? I don't see anyone in the meadow. Quite right. They could see tiny paths along the grass made from the recent tramping of size 0000002 shoes, but the owners of the shoes were nowhere to be seen.

Very strange, thought Turnipseed. Very Strange. But then she saw the King lollygagging about by taking a short snooze under a large, ageing mushroom which cast out a gigantic shadow as refuge from the days heat. Gigantic, at least, to a fairy, an eight inch high pig, and to Lars his royalness.

Lars was not snoozing for he jumped up and waved frantically at the approaching duo. "Halloo!" he yelled. "Halloo! I am here!"

Turnipseed clasped her hands together, for it was the proper thing to do to show excitement and still is when one is being hallooed! "Halloo yourself, for we see you fine and clearly, but we seem to be amiss at seeing your earnest crew!"

"That's easy to explain. You can't see them because they're not here! Simple as that. I sent them home -- since I'm with you, you can use your powers which stay through the sunlight to protect you and I..."

"Me..." she corrected. "Protect you and ME!"

"Let's not waste time quibbling, Turnipseed. They are in perilous positions here, because their power is only good at night..."

"So we think," she corrected. "No one ever knows for sure, because they have never been known to test the daytime, have they?"

"Shall we have a debate about daytime powers, Turnipseed? Or shall we get on with the task at hand -- to find Brimble? And by the way, hallo -- it's Bartholomew, is it?"

"I prefer Barty, your majestic highness."

"Well, you certainly have that right, I do admit, though I reckon you're the only tiny pig I have ever met." He smiled, and muttered to himself, "How did they get a pig so damn tiny."

Turnipseed broke in. "How did we get you and me to be so damn tiny? Put that in your pipe and smoke it, Lars."

"Some things are private property, and thoughts ought to be one of them, " Lars said aloud.

"Here, here, " Barty said. "Here, here!"

"Oh bosh, the two of you probably rarely have an intelligent thought between you if each took a half shot at it!"

"Probably rarely?" replied the king.

"Oh, she's exquisite with the split participle, you know, your esteemed one. She works on splitting them day and night, hunting elephants in her Pajamas, you know?"

"How does an elephant ever fit into her Pajamas? You're tiny granted, but an elephant..."

Tumbleweed gave a seemingly irritated look at Lars, but she was enjoying this part.

"I see you never watch the Marx brothers, Lars. Anyway, we best hurry. I imagine that every moment we waste, something is more apt to happen to Brimble."

Lars was hesitant and did not easily go into that bright day.

"Lars...for heaven's sake, put yourself right here. We can't keep wasting all this time or Brimble could be in serious problems right now, Lars. Let's go." He still stood looking at Turnipseed and Barty even after the direct invitation. Turnipseed continued, " Now, I am not going there on my own power so I'm riding Barty, and I know you think you don't have any powers in the sunlight, so you also will have to ride Barty with me. But for heaven's sake, we've got to do something. Now I'm riding Bartholomew, and so shall you!"

"You know, Turnipseed...I...I...I'm not all that comfortable with heights!"

"You fly almost every night, Kingship dear. So don't give me that hogslop! No offense, Barty."

"But it's dark, and I can't see down -- and when it's moonlight, I don't look down."

"Lars, get on Barty, and put your hands around my waist, and just hold tight. I won't let you fall!"

Delicately, Lards slide his breeched leg over Barty's broad back, and when settled, clasped his arms about Turnipseed's dainty waist.

"My, oh my, oh my!" Turnipseed thought, and turned ahead to make sure that Lars could not see her flustered smile.

Lars had never been this close to Turnipseed before and did not expect his heart to race just so slightly. "Jonathan and Delicious," he said aloud without much prior thought.

Turnipseed was so intent on getting her thought to Barty that she hardly realized the King had spoken, but Tooth Faeries if anything are decidedly polite. (If they are in your room, and you sneeze, why they will always say Genzundheit! Sometimes, you can even hear the salutation as you use a hanky to wipe your nose before falling back fast asleep)

"Bartletts, too," thought the King. "And walnuts and pecans! What an interesting perfume. But it is wonderful scent."

Turnipseed's smile grew large and warm. She wanted to say something, but one doesn't always insist on notifying her company that she knows what they are thinking.

Instead, she asked aloud, very civilly, but with a new silvered-bell daintiness, "Where are we going, Lars?"

"Well, I can't see the stars in the daylight, you know, so navigations going to be difficult, but I think the first stop should be at the gold storage and see if Brimble might be there -- safe, or I hate to think of this, in harm's way! You've never been there, have you, Turnipseed? Have you?"

"I have a vague Idea, King!" Could it be precisely at 65 degrees one minute latitude and 41º 88' N, 87º 63' at 586 feet above sea level? That's my rough guess."

And of course, she was precise down to the freckle on a fly's back!

Chapter 4

The Sergeant was right!

It was Lodi that he had heard, but where he had not been able to recount to the king and the group of faeries. Now she sat in the Snake's Turning on the Ascot neighborhood "public ale house" or 'pub' as they are called in London. Alongside her sat Alexandroweiscz, her favorite frog and mount, and both she and Addie were having a "foamy" -- a non-alcoholic blend of whatever the brew master had to work with. He had found five pounds of roots and ginger, and made a delicious concoction not too unlike our root beer. Frankly, Lodi preferred fruit drinks, but the frog, being a frog, preferred things that were musky and basementy in smell and taste, and was such a spoiled creature that he refused the free drinks unless they were all this "foamy".

Although Lodi was not truly a faerie, she looked one. However, she had no wings, nor, for that matter did she really need them, for she had the gift of flight without wings. And instead of wearing diaphanous, revealing dresses as did the faeries for the most part, she wore tights and leggings and had green shirt that she cinched with a tight belt around her tinier waist. That outlined her most feminine figure, which she topped out with a small handmade cap perkily balanced against her short-cropped hair.

She felt cheated that they were meeting without her in the next room. She could smell the smell of cold cigar smoke and hear the different creatures. She could only understand the Lizards, for the Snake King was more hiss than talk -- his sibilant consonants slid long into oblivion. The tones were not precise and chopped as yours are or are mine. But a snake, lacking savoir faire, tried to be flattering and deceiving with the soothing vowels and buttered consonants that seemed to oil their way around the room. They sat either on a cushion by the table in the corner (mostly the snakes, who could not sit) and the lizards. Their clothes were dark and earth-colored giving them perfect camouflage that allowed them to slink about undetected amide the shadows and the foliage. They were villainous and cold-blooded creatures -- literally. And that is why their paths and the little people rarely overlapped. But Lodi was neither day nor night, but she as a sprite inhabited that time between the day and the night, when nothing is quite as it should be, and far worse enemies of good lurk about looking for the hapless who are caught in the day or those of the day who venture too long into the darkness.

Addie (don't you think that is a wonderful diminutive of Alexandroweiscz, which after all, is 15 letters long, and even then, Addie was never quite certain which order each letter was organized in) was also cold blooded, and very much an amphibian. He was also extremely very nervous being in the same Pub as the Snake King. He constantly was moving about, keeping his eyes on the doorway, and the other on the window, planning, as it were, a fast exit for any contingency with the snake. Lizards? He was not sure. Snakes, he was deathly sure.

"Lodi," he said, after taking a long sip. It is entirely too still in here -- listen. See? No noise, no whispering . There aren't even any drunks laughing."

"It's daytime, Addie! Of course it's quiet, because the only ones in here are losers! Or they would be at work or at home getting ready to work. What? You're afraid that mean ole snake's going to come through that door over there and get you? For what, dinner? We've brought them a long way if only to have all the little rodents and reptilians like you for the rest of their lives' So why would you think they would make you supper today and blow that?"

"I am an amphibian — not a brainless reptile," Addie interjected. "There's a big difference!"

The frog looked again at the door before turning back to Lodi and to the thread of thought. "Because their very nature says that I'm dinner, and they can't change their nature, Lodi. I don't trust them!"

The swinging door opened and the first in was the Lizard. Now in real life, lizards are prone to walk on all four feet. But you have seen the nature shows that show they really can get up on their back two legs and run, their tails waiving back and forth like a willow switch behind them. The lizard king long ago had mastered that during a run, when thinking about it, he surmised that he could actually slow down and still stay erect. This gave him a chance to observe things other lizards have not been able to, and that is how he began to realize that books have words and pages, which one cannot fathom at all when one's nose is only a half inch from the type. However, and this is the just of intelligence for all creatures, when one has a superior view, one can soon see the pattern of letters and begin to read! And for a lizard, any lizard at all, that is something so phenomenal that it becomes the defining difference between just hiding out in a sandhole or being able to understand the masters and wear fine brocaded silks and luxurious worsted! That is precisely how he had become king -- because he could read the tattered pages of all the newspapers and magazines he would encounter upon the way.

The snake king, on the other hand, would always be what he was at the very minute -- able to only slither upon the ground, and every so often, rise above all, such as his distant cousin, the cobra. Just very little, however. For the snake king was a fat blow snake who had overcome all his pretenders (basically by making

them long meals) and was now looked at in awe by snake and non-snake enough. He slid into the main room of the pub just minutes after the lizard.

The snake hissed first. "S-s-s-oo! You have Brimble, I understand. V-e-e-r-r-ry g-o-o-od. "He made his way to the bar counter, and slid upon the top, where his face was level with Lodi and Addie. Addie immediately moved to put Lodi between himself and the frog.

"Tell the frog that I am not hungry, he need not hide!"

Addie spoke under his breath to Lodi, "I must say, Lodi, that declarative does little to subdue my untrusting nature! As the saying goes, one does not gamble with the Devil!"

The snakes head drew again once more on an even plane with the Frog, but then slid away again.

The snake slid onto a barstool, then had the bartender draw a bitter and place before him, where one of the snakes many lizard servants gave the king snake a drink. The snake king then wiped his mouth with his long tongue. "There is a usefulness to all things, what?" He said, and gave a hissy type of laugh. "Now then, the nature of the visit, I understand is this. You have Brimble somewhere and you are willing to let us then to do what is necessary to get Brimble to lead us to the gold, is that right? You know, that will probably mean that we will have to perhaps break a bone or amputate a finger to get Brimble to, shall we say, cooperate?"

"No!" Lodi did not fear the Snake king, for like the faerie queen, Turnipseed, somehow she had the ability to keep her special powers in night or day -- and to Frog, she had also left enchantment, as Turnipseed had to Barty!. "That is nowhere near what we are agreeing to do! There is enough gold there to more than be enough to you and your kingdom and to the Faerie

Kingdom! I am merely saying that we make a deal with Brimble to, shall we say, share the wealth? I do get tired, you see, of constantly having to genuflect to the king every time that I wish to have some coin for uses. And I no longer steal, so I have to ask when I like! Brimble can be a most compromising leprechaun!"

"Ah, but is not using Brimble to, as you say, compromise, shall we say, it is very much like stealing?"

"I think that Brimble is a reasonable leprechaun, sir!"

"Reasonable now you say? You have already said Compromise. Shall we say? Indeed? One does seem like the other, for only the naming is different!"

"Not so," protested Lodi. "How then did the kingdom get the gold but by the taking from the poor minors before they had a chance to keep it?"

"You mean, find it?" said the snake. "I see your reasoning, though flawed it might be. " He took another sip and wiped his lips again. "What you are saying, then, is that if we take something that was found, not earned, then it is not stealing, but rather re-finding? What a delicious way to avoid facing what others considered the truth?"

"I beg your pardon, Snake. I no longer can steal by agreement with the King Faerie! But if we leave more gold than we take -- there is that much there and so much more. It will not be missed!"

So you say -- but how do we explain Brimble? Unless we kill him? And if we kill him there is no need to take just part of the gold."

"The lizard king, who had set before him a "foamie" objected. "I do not like the thought of killing Brimble at all, for then we shall have the entire faerie complex to deal with. And that thought is frightful!"

"Of course, I w-a-s-s-s-s just thinking. Of course, we don't kill Brimble, for Brimble is a nice lad, though easily drunk, I agree!"

"You don't need to ever kill a drunk, for what can a true sot ever remember anyway?" Lodi asked.

Addie was already into his third foamie. "More than you realize," he said, under his breath.,

Thankfully the Snake did not hear him well, although the lizard did slightly nod his agreement.

"This is all very interesting, but there is one thing that might change the whole of this, Lodi. What if we don't need you to make this, shall we say, agreement work? In other words, what if we already have Brimble?"

"No, I don't buy that one minute, your Snakiness! Firstly, we have hidden Brimble very securely that you won't be able to find him..."

"Was he drunk?"

"Possibly close, I believe!"

The snake hissed his hideous laugh again, and placed his face directly in front of the Frog. "Addie knows when I say, 'One's nature does not change! Aye, friend frog? A drunk might not remember, but I doubt that. But a drunken leprechaun rarely will stay hid long. What would you say if I told you that Brimble had walked here of his own accord, or been, shall we say, invited?"

"Whenever you say, shall we say, there seems to be a deceit!" Lodi said.

Her answer was another hissing laugh from the Snake.

Just at that moment, they heard a muffled yell. Both Lodi and Addie looked down to the floor until any hint of yelling had ceased. Then Lodi turned to Addie. "This isn't going as I thought it would!"

"Does it ever?" Addie answered, and his hand was so shaken, the as he put it onto the counter, it spilt nearly half the contents onto the Snake, whose eyes narrowed into slits.

"Did you want to stay for the good part? Say, dinner?"

With that, and just a leap ahead of the Snake's lizard Guard, Addie and Lodi burst outside and were immediately airborne. It had come so swiftly and without warning, that Addie had a frightful scratch where a lizards hands had raked down his skin. Addie separated from Lodi, then headed back to where she hovered in the air over the pub.

"Don't you dare harm Brimble!" she yelled. All that could be heard as a reply was a full throated laugh from the lizard, and a long, drawn-out hissing laugh from the Snake king.

Chapter 5

The Defenders Fight!

"According to my calculations, we should be just about there, Lars. There's a large wild olive ahead..."

There was not response, so she looked behind her. "This is the funniest trip I have ever taken. I have the king of all faerieland behind me -- a man who flies every night on his own. Yet here we are, and he's afraid of the heights!" she thought. Then said she aloud, "Lars, open your eyes, or I'll never find the gold!"

In response, she felt his hands encircling her waist tighten perceptively.

"OK, Turnipseed! I have them opened, but a fat lot of good it is doing me, what with your veil hitting my face with the wind!" He let go with one hand, and wiped away the veil. "It looks different in the daytime. I'm not certain whether that's it, Turnipseed... Can you go down and hover? I don't come out here often, you know. I just have Brimble or Skinny bring back what I need."

They stood in the air, perhaps 100 feet up for just a moment before the king spotted it. "There is Brimble and Skinny's nighttime cottage, all right, so we're at the right place."

An Irish cottage stood hidden by brush, but the white of its' whitewashed side sparkled in the sunlight. Turnipseed nudged Barty and the trio descended to the cottage. Before Barty's feet had touched the ground, the king lept off, his feet finally back on solid earth.

Turnipseed didn't see danger, but something told her to move Barty into the brush.

"Lars!" she stage whispered. "Get back here. What if they're still here?"

Lars turned around and jumped into the bush by Turnipseed. "What if who's still here?" he asked. "Oh, you're right. I'll look around. Stay here, tune in my thoughts -- I'll let you know if there is anything dangerous. The gold's hidden in a little cavern to the north of the cottage. I'll let you know when it's all clear."

Turnipseed said nothing. As soon as the King was out of sight, she cloaked herself with invisibility, and set out to follow the King. He might have no daylight powers, but she did. She motioned Barty to remain quiet. "I'll be ok -- you stay out of sight."

It did not take the King long to scout the cottage and find, to his relief that it was empty. Yet, he had also wished that it were inhabited by Brimble.

On entering the cottage, Lars observed that everything looked quite right. The telly sat in the corner of the room. It was large and old, obviously rescued from a thrift shop, and setting on a crocheted doily, a hanger wire with pods of tinfoil served quite adequately as its antenna. There were no bedrooms, but a comfortable and frayed old sofa served nicely whenever a nap was needed. The sink and dishes were washed and tidy. Certainly, no harm or ill will had taken place here!

The king returned outside, carefully and quietly closing the door behind him. He could see the brush that masqueraded the opening to the cave with the Pot O' Gold. Really, it was more like a dug-out that he had helped scrape from the hillside, and had proven to be more than adequate.

A dank smell of earth was very noticeable, for water still seeped along the floor of the cavern and had washed most of the dirt down to the pebbles of this antediluvian hill left when an ancient river had dried. There also was a new smell that he could not place, but since he could not identify it, he would ignore it but be twice careful. Turnipseed watched from a distance which allowed her to watch Lars and not reveal herself to the king because of her fruity scent.

Brimble and Skinny were really 12 year-old boys at heart in the bodies of 700 year old Leprechauns. Which meant that they liked to play and joke around. None of their pranks were malevolent, but they often would spend more time playing games and staying past their time in the pubs with their friends. They did, however, take very seriously their duty to protect the gold. That is how they first got the idea of having help in guarding the gold. They had met Freddie and his buddy, Tommy near their cottage one night and offered the two strangers a nice long drink of bitters. "Come to our little cottage for the drink. We'd like to talk to you about some things." And one thing led to the other. That is why the King was in some jeopardy, for inside the cavern were Freddie and his buddy, Tommy. They were both asleep, and if they knew who Lars was, they would certainly have set out to entertain him differently than they did that day.

Lars squinched his brows and squeezed his eyes shut. "Turnipseed, I am at the entrance to the cave. So far so good. I have not seen anything or anyone. Perhaps we're over-reacting to Brimble's absence; everything seems very ordinary." With that, he brushed aside the hanging camouflage canvas that hid the opening to the cave. The musty odor nearly caused him to reconsider entering, but he took a big breath and stepped inside. It was dark and in the dark he thought he heard noises. Almost it sounded like a slow, even breathing, could it be Brimble? He listened for a moment, and concluded that his senses were too expectant of something bad happening. The sound had disappeared.

He stealthily took his bearing and continued walking. The cauldron should be nearby. It was full-sized, for after all, the coins were not miniature, they too were full sized. So it would not take much to find the cauldron. Again he heard a noise; he did not realize that an invisible Turnipseed was following him in.

Freddie had been asleep but a smell quickly brought him to full consciousness. He nudged Tommy, but Tommy was totally asleep, and nothing would awaken him, it would seem. So Freddie decided to investigate. Freddie was very nearsighted, as most tarantula's are, but he also had little fear, so he would investigate. The smell was -- different. A little fruity. Like apples? Silly. Ridiculous. But then, pears? Something was there.

Turnipseed stopped short. She could see the outline of Lars, but she heard a scurrying, like a rat would make. Rats! Mice, they were gentlemen. But Rats?

Lars smelt the spider before he saw it. Or rather felt it. For as he held out his hand he felt the hairy front leg of the spider. It moved! His initial reaction was to run, but he felt he should stay absolutely still.

The spider immediately felt the vibration of the King's touch. He too froze. It would move again, he was certain, then he would pounce! He did not exhale but stood poised to strike..

Turnipseed caught the fright Lars was experiencing. She could not see the spider, but she knew the fear, and could even hear Lars heart heaving.

Lars tiptoed to the side and his hand reached out and touched the cauldron. "Well, I have found the cauldron,

Turnipseed, "he thought. But there is something very terrible here with me. And I have no powers!" He kept creeping trying to put the cauldron -- anything between him and the spider. Again he heard the scurry of the spider's feet as it shuffled about trying to find him.

Tommy had also smelled the fruit. Actually, he was not a fruit creature, but this was an odd scent mixture, all full of walnuts and apples -- and pears! And he could see -- for scorpions see very well in the dark, thank you, for they are creatures that you find in the darkest places of all! There was a little man coming toward him. And not at all a Leprechaun like his friends Brimble and Skinny, for this creature coming round the cauldron had not the pointed ears and funny clothing that he now expected all Leprechauns to have. Tommy raised his tail with its deadly tip and began to stealthily move toward the little man. He would take just a few steps then stop.

Where was Freddie when he needed him? Normally he could smell the tarantula, because the spider, being who he was, was not terrible hygienic. Past food clung to his leg hairs like bits of flotsam that stick to men's beards. He knew this scent was not Freddie because the smell was of fresh fruit and nuts and was heady and overwhelming.

Lars could hear both the spider scurrying about and a new sound. It seemed to be an exhale from another creature far closer than he guessed the spider to be. But what was this creature? Or the spider for that matter. He wanted to yell out, but could not. For after all, these could be the very creatures that had captured Brimble. Perhaps Brimble was even tied up. Before he could finish that thought, something very sticky had shot out about him, and he found himself being wrapped, and giant hands seemed to be turning him round and round. He was absolutely trapped in something.

"Tommy! I've got something! Wake up!"

"I see -- I'm right by you. It's a small man -- like Brimble!"

"So you have Brimble! " The king was seething, but trapped as he was, he could still talk.

"I beg your pardon, governor. Have Brimble? I should say not! Who are you?"

With that question, the room began to glow. Turnipseed was filling the room with faerie power!

"That, gentlemen, is the king of Faeries, may I introduce King Larceus. And I think that I have escaped having the charm of knowing who you are? And what are you doing here?"

Quick as that, Freddie ripped the silken threads from Lars. Once free, Lars just sat with his head propped by his hand. "I thought I was a dead man!"

"And well you should have thought so," said Tommy. " For if Freddie there had not had you for dinner tonight, I well should have thought about it! What are you doing in this cave today, your Kingship!. It is not good for you little people to be about on a sunlit day, for then ye have no power! And who are ye, grand lady of the light?"

I like that -- Grande Lady of the Light! I am Turnipseed -- the tooth faerie!"

Freddie guffawed. "Turnipseed? Like the seed of a Turnip, you don't say?"

"Gentlemen -- for I perceive you to be such, we are on a desperate mission. Brimble is missing!"

"Oh, that does take a different road, doesn't it, your highness," Freddie said. "Because for a fortnight, we haven't set eyes on him. Ole Skinny was here by himself for about an hour last night, but then he left quickly. Never said a word. Just left. I don't recollect anyone being with him. We just looked out at the commotion and figured he was worried. We never saw Brimble, though. That we did not."

Freddie came over to the king. "Look, your majesty, Tommy and I don't get out a lot, you see, because we are disconcertin' to most other creatures..."

Tommy broke in to finish the thought, "...cause our kind – well, we have a bad habit of eaten' creatures, we do. But we're kind hearten. We onliest kills because we can get powerfully hungry! But we never kills or eats little people or those creatures you've enchanted. It goes against our policy all the way!

Freddie continued. "Anyway, Brimble is one of our best friends. We would gladly join your excursion, and I know I speak for Tommy, too ...But there are some things that we can do, I reckon, about as good as anyone. For our sizes, we both are remarkably agile and can slip around, behind, under and sometimes through most anything put on earth. And except that we occasionally kill and eat things, we're both kind-hearted and mutually desirous of helping out a friend of our friend. Oh, and you needn't worry, there's nothing missing of the gold here. You're the first person besides Brimble and Skinny Kenneth that's ever been this side of the canvass, your honors!"

Chapter 6

Lodi Repents

Lodi and Addie perched in a tall Sycamore whose gnarled exposed tree roots formed a knee that acted as a natural shelter for the pub. They were safely away, but now the danger was very real below.

"Addie, I had no idea they would get Brimble. I thought we hid him very well." She said. She was sitting, and her legging covered calf dropped below the leaf line. But it was very green. And she was very safe.

"Drunks can walk. Brimble probably walked himself right to the pub. Do you think he's going to see us up here?" Addie asked.

"Hardly. Snakes and Lizards usually do not think of looking up. It's their nature, you know, to look for things their own level. I think they're coming out -- and I think they're going to head right toward the Gold! I wish we knew where it was so we could get there first. Perhaps then we could do something to help Brimble! You know, he cannot stand direct sunlight, he is so perfect of complexion, he will immediately go into heatstroke. That's what legend has it, that Brimble's father who is Skinny Kenneth's uncle actually died of heatstroke when he stay up till the sun was present!"

Addie spoke after listening to Lodi go on. "Any ideas?"

She sagged as she spoke, "None...none at all! But we must come up with something...we must save Brimble!"

"Your mind is a-jumble, Lodi." The frog turned to look once more below. I imagine they will head that way, but is Brimble going to last till they get there? They can't fly, remember. So it's slither and walk all the way.

The snake king was doing quite well, for he was oiled to slip along through the paths of the grass. You and I being the big ones that we are, do not even know of all the little pathways that snakes and mice and the elves use. For they are like paved highways for little creatures who have used them for millennium through the meadows and grasslands and forests. It is vexing to them when some big folk decides to plow and plant, even a garden or a flower patch, for then they must use their other senses to decide where a path or small road should be set to closely resemble the prior one. That way, they can enter the rearranged area where they normally do, and if all goes well, come out on the other side in about the same place.

If we were to get down on a high lawn so that our cheek lay along the ground, we could hear the soft footsteps of the little ones and peer in on their goings and comings along these little by-ways. In fact, I have done that on certain afternoons that were just blending into evening and nightfall, that wonderful time when the enchanted ones first begin to scurry about. In fact, I did meet the Sergeant once, who really is my only source for this story I am telling you, though he swears upon his soul that it did happen. And a mouse who swears upon his soul should be listened to attentively. You will not meet many, I dare say, who are willing to thus swear!

Let me get back to the story! Lodi and Addie had headed for the height of the trees to keep watchful over Brimble.

The King was enjoying the excursion for he was swinging back and forth, back and forth as snakes must do to travel. But it is like a dance to the snakes, who soon become nearly hypnotized by the movement of it all and enjoy it enormously so. In fact, they have been known to go far further than they really needed. That's what the rhythm was like that day to the King Snake. Everyone else was griping about the distance. They griped about the heat. They griped about having to go at all, when all those fellows really preferred to be back at the pub.

The lizard king had a unique method of walking to, which he also rather enjoyed. For as his left front foot would come forward (remember, he walked about on his back feet only, but he did always have to take into consideration that his giant tail would swish in the opposite direction of his advancing foot, so always he had to turn his shoulders extremely the same direction. He therefore gave the impression that he was doing that old American Dance from the Mid-Century, called the twist.

He began to hum the Twisting song. Being somewhat a dimwit, at least compared to the snake King, he never could remember someone else's words, so he made his up. And he sang today.

"Let's twist again. Like we did at Aunt Martha's!

"Let's twist again. Like we did in your...

Backyard....Oh! Oh! Oh!"

The Snake King did not care what words were sung, though he did feel the Lizard had an exemplary baritone voice. So he swished back and forth in time with the song. He had reason to be happy, too. He had Brimble. He slowed down and let the first part of the procession by, and slid into step by Brimble.

"We could make this-s-s-s-s much easier on you Brimble. After all, we're not mean-hearten. What would you like? Water? Catnip tea? A cold soda. A cold brew or foamie?" He laughed at his remarkable gesture of amiability. "We could all go home right away, Brimble. It's up to you. You could just tell us where that cauldron is and we would fetch some of it by ourselves and save you this hot, hot, ho-o-o-o-t walk." He looked up at the sun, now filtering through the tree canopy of leaves, letting the light splash golden along the route in little splotches on the green. "Oh, look, look Brimble," he added. "Look at that beautiful sun there! Why, I imagine that it's more HOT out there!"

"I am still a'drunk, kingey snake -- but I will NEVER let anyone near me gold! I guards it from every creature, especially the likes of your sniveling little tongue and beady eyes. You can throw me into that sun, and I'll melt in a moment -- or die. And you know, I've lived a thousand or so years, so I've already done a lot of livin' and I ain't afraid of dying fore I'll let some yellow-bellied SNAKE rob us little 'uns BLIND!" Brimble could be tempestous at times, and whenever he did, he always spoke in BIG HUGE CAPITAL letters! No snake was going to push him on this!

"Brimble, to show you I'm not as bad as you think I am, I want you to have a sip of this!" The snake had his porter open a child's baby bottle, which was full of water. "I won't have any gold unless I keep you alive till we find the gold. So I need you to drink one or two swallows of this -- it's just good water, Brimble. Do be so kind as to drink this!"

Brimble took the water, eyed the snake warily and tilted back his head and loaded his mouth with water. But he didn't swallow. Instead he held the bottle upside down and let all the droplets fall into the dry earth, where it formed a little dusty droplet before it was sucked into ground. And he turned to the snake king and SPAT the mouthful on the snake.

"I don't need your water -- you can go to!"

The king's eyes filled quickly with a flash of hate, and his whole body rocked into the air, and he bared his fangs, which quickly pointed out and down, ready for a lunge. He stood poised in the air but then the stiffness went back out of him; his body relaxed and lay upon the ground, flat.

Brimble stared at the King. "If ye have vile plans to do me in, then be quick about it and save yourself a trip to no-where, because I will not show you the way! So get it done now!"

The Snake King practically purred, and wrapped his self about Brimble, in a cascade of scales.

"Brimble, Brimble, Brimble! What say I about "do you in"? I dare say, but did I mention anything of the sort? "

"You inferred it..."

"So say ye! But I did not, so be calm! " The column began to move again. "There is so much gold there, I have been told by those who helped build the fortune. A huge pot -- big people sized --that is filled to brimming with gold pieces. There certainly has to be enough there for everyone, not just you little people! The rest of us? We only want what is our fair share! You help us get what's coming to us, and there is certainly not going to be any suffering! Or hurt by any creature, including you!"

"Fair Share?" Brimble repeated. "Your share? I don't think so. You haven't done anything deserving of a single gold coin, yet you talk about your fair share? What did you ever do to deserve a fair share?"

The king Snake shrugged as well as he could as a snake. "Do? Indeed, indeed! It's a pity you got rid of your water -- whatever shall you do when we go into the Sun?"

Lodi flitted about in the trees. As I said -- or have I? -- it has been so long since I could visit with the little people that I might have already begun to forget what they have told me! -- Lodi had all the powers that Turnipseed possessed except for one. She did not have the power to cloak herself with invisibility. At night, as I know I have said, she did have the power to be invisible to those who could harm her. And that invisibility included a cloaking of herself to all the senses of others. In the daytime, the sprites generally had their powers of flight and a few odds and ends tucked away such as throwing their voices, not just through ventriloquism, but actually having their voices heard from a spot different than the spot spoken from, and the ability to become very small (even to the little people!) And Lodi could make Addie also become very, very tiny like unto herself.

She said to Addie: "I could make you and I very tiny and go down among them. Perhaps that shan't see us and we shall be safe."

"Or become dinner, "Addie finished her sentence -- somewhat! "At that size, we shall be perfect morsels for both the snakes and Lizards, and I count twenty of them. I would feel like a Pinball machine if we have to face those odds at that size!"

Lodi laughed, and swung about a branch to slingshot her to a higher branch.

"Oh, you are fast, Addie! Such a   boobie!"

"I know that snake King will have me for lunch if we do that...what we need, Lodi, is backup!"

"Backup! The others will hate me for what I have done! We need to do this ourselves!"

Addie had landed on the elbow of a branch of a large Oak and hid behind a sucker so that if any of the reptilian herd below were to look upwards they would not be able to locate him in the tree. "What do you want? Your pride intact or Brimble intact? Addie peered about, still not convinced they were alone. "You go back and find your two sisters and any other creature you can find and bring them back to help us. I'll stay in the trees. So look for me when you return!"

Lodi hesitated for only a moment, then yelled, "Keep watch -- follow them. I will bring anyone I can find to help us, Addie!" And she flitted away, like a dainty dragonfly on a whiff of a soft summer breeze.

The king was already behind Turnipseed on Barty, his arms locked tightly about her as Barty began to rise above the terrain. The large spider and the tarantula looked far less foreboding now, not just because of their somewhat dubious kind nature, but also because they became smaller and smaller as the pig rose. The two on the ground waved an array of legs or other appendages at the two on the pig.

"I think that I rather like those two, "the king said.

"I think that I rather like those two, too. On the ground. Down there. I don't think I could fathom the thought of either of those riding up here and then deciding to act the nature of the creature."

"Oh, Barty," Tumbleweed cried. I would rescue you!"

"But it would be after the fact, Tumbleweed," said Barty. I have a theory about certain creatures. They might genuinely be happy to see us, and genuinely want to help Brimble. But if you stay around creatures too long, it is a natural law that they revert to their natural selves. And that is because 24 hours a day, they are who they are. It only takes a slip of a few seconds -- say they were to have a piggy pie or something, that is their natural way. So they are good for hours, and only are they natural for a few minutes, but those few minutes do make a case for the prosecution!

Chapter 7

Gathering at the Meadow

Sergeant Mouse and his wife's home was a cozy cottage that he had built into the bluff by the small creek that ran through the north side of the meadow. It was high enough above the high water mark that in thirty years it had never had a drop of water enter into the home. So he had been able to plaster the walls and ceiling with a beautiful white and blue pastel that lit up the room with just the help of a lamp he had made from the light bulb and batteries of a lost flashlight and part of an old brass candle holder.

His family thought him to be the most creative and imaginative mouse that ever lived, and not being acquainted with many enchanted mouses (remember the plural!), I have a distinct impression that they are right.

Mrs. Sergeant (really -- I don't want to give away her name, or she will be besieged with all sorts of autograph seekers and probably even reporters from The Star!) had lovingly prepared a fine meal of millet seed and cold roast beef that she kept cool in the cistern house by the creek. He doused the whole meal with a big cup of homemade apple cider. After dinner, he sat in his wonderfully big and fluffy easy chair and to the strains of Vivaldi, attempted to catch up on some reading. But the thought of Brimble, missing, wherever, was too much for him to let sleep slip in. As he sat in his quilted robe, he said a silent prayer that Brimble would be alright.

He did not arise when a knocking was heard at the door. He watched with some interest as his wife answered the door. He could not see past her to discern the visitor, but he could hear the high feminine voice on the other side. He heard his wife say, "I just think the Sergeant is too tired to go out again. He's tried all he could..." and the voice on the other side said something. Then his wife turned back to the Sergeant.

"It's Princess MorningStar, Dear. "

"Well, ask her in, dear! By all means, don't leave her out in the daylight!" And saying that, he arose, and went to meet her just as MorningStar burst into the room, her breath coming in quick, noisy droughts.

"I've been to everyone I can think of, Sergeant! Of course, the trolls can't come because they blow up in daylight, you see! But there are many people gathering not far from here to help find Brimble. We haven't heard from the King or Turnipseed...but if we don't do something right now, Brimble can die from the heat! We need your leadership! And -- since you're an enchanted creature, you have no power's to lose except that your scent can be detected. But there are hundreds outside, so there should be safety in numbers!"

The sergeant tweaked away a tear from the corner of his eye. That so many of the little people were willing to place their lives in jeopardy to save one person, it was absolutely overwhelming to him.

He turned to his wife. "Dear -- I must go..."

A few minutes later a roar went up from the assembly. It was a tiny roar as far as roars go to the Big People, but a huge roar to the little ones!. The sergeant looked over the lot -- elves, faeries, sprites! Of course, no Leprechauns or Trolls, for they would not have any chance at living if they were to join the group. But everyone else was there, save for the plump little mothers who must stay with their children.

Presently the group formed in ranks of two with the Sergeant and the Princess MorningStar at advance. The sergeant, shielding his mouth so only MorningStar could hear, whispered to her, "Where are we to go exactly? Do you have any ideas?"

None of us know where the Cauldron is hidden, but I believe that it is somewhere toward the South foothills, and I think that is the way to head right now. We'll stay in the roadways (Remember that these are the roads of Tiny People that we earlier talked about) through the meadows. We shouldn't be seen then -- especially by the owls and such, if any hunt during the day. I believe that we will have good covering of grass and weeds and bushes and such. We must be on the guard against cats and snakes, Sergeant."

The Sergeant turned aside. "I'll post the rest of the mouses along the Expedition Column to keep our flanks safe, Princess. Lead away! I'll return after I have set them up!" And soon there were 15 enchanted mouses posted every twenty feet along the column to offer as much safety as possible to the group. Then the Sergeant returned to his position by MorningStar.

I would like to tell you that there were no dangers, but there were. Flying above the group were several dragonflies that MorningStar had enlisted. With their complex eyes, they were able to see in back, in front, to each side and below all at once! Suddenly, each dived to the column below.

The lead Dragonfly reported directly to MorningStar. "There are some hawks ahead who have seen the movement of the grass from the column! They are flying this way -- so everyone! Freeze! And just pray they don't see any!"

Sweat rolled off the faces of nearly every Expeditionary as they saw the hawks circle overhead. They had read about the amazing vision of the hawks, and dared not move or it seemed, to breathe, until they saw the birds start circling more to the north and leave them out of danger. Even then they waited several minutes before resuming their course.

Lodi found most of the homes empty, but she thumped on door to door to find someone home. After thumping on one door, it was opened by a tiny little boy elf, and immediately it was slammed shut again by a plump little mother elf.

"Wait! Don't shut the door! It's me -- Lodi!"

"That's why I shut the door! Go away, Lodi! You Traitor...you conniving traitor! You Meshugana Sprite! (Yes, elves were of all faiths). Get away from my doorstoop!"

"I'm trying to help! I don't want Brimble to be hurt -- they promised they wouldn't hurt him, but they are going to! I need help to get Brimble back safely!"

Mrs. Chubby Elf Mother slowly opened the door. "How could you sell your own kind for some Gold?"

"I told you -- I didn't mean any harm to come to him. I don't have time to explain. I just need to find everyone to get them to help save Brimble!"

"I shouldn't do this -- you have an evil eye, Lodi!" So saying, she spit twice..." The truth of the matter? I don't know where they are -- they're on an Expedition is all I know, going South through the meadow last as I saw of them-- nearly everyone except we mothers with small children. You go help them. Save Brimble! We'll talk about the rest some other time. You owe it!" This time the door shut more softly, but still with as much finality as before.

"Princess MorningStar. We don't have a plan or a clue of where we are going. Have you formulated any kind of plan at all?"

"Frankly, Sergeant, I am simply thinking that if we do nothing, nothing at all will come of this. But that if we just do something -- anything at all, something will happen. We have more chance of finding Brimble by doing something, even if we just think that we are marching forward."

"Yes, I suppose. I suppose." but now, the sergeant's tone was less believable.

The Snake King hissed for the group to stop. "I see something is amiss above, " he hissed. "For I have seen a shadow, and methinks it looks awfully like a...dare I say it? A frog. Above us, I dare say. Like a flying frog. Come," he motioned for the others. "Come along, children, let us go along. After all, what can one frog do?" The group kept along, but presently, as they came to a clump of orchard glass, the king motioned to the Lizard to halt. In this position, he was certain that the frog had no view of the group. The king said nothing, but with his head, motioned the group that he, the King Snake was going to explore.

It was after five or ten minutes that Addie deducted that the group below was resting, and having been awake for nearly eight hours himself (which is a dreadfully long time for a Frog not to take a siesta) he set about to remedy the situation himself, and soon loud froggy snores croaked away into the summer's air.

He jumped as he felt something, but settled back into his slumber before awakening with a start. He was staring into the eyes of the Snake King! "Hello, little morsel -- dinner, shall we say?" crooned the Snake King.

Addie applied torque to his froggy legs to launch himself, then realized that the king's valets held him firmly to the tree. Indeed, they had thrown a net around, and tied the net to the tree!

The king Snake spoke again. "Are we keeping some kind of watch by day, sir Frog? My, I don't see your friend Lodi suddenly. Has she become smacked with remorse for our little deal?"

Addie was shaking with fear. His idea that morning certainly was not to become dinner to a monarch. Still, his heart felt strong, and he could sense the adrenalin surge through his little heart

"I'm not afraid of you, Snake!"

"Oh! No title when addressing royalty? " The Snake's voice immediately turned dark and evil-sounding. "I would be afraid, if you are afraid of being invited to dinner, as, shall we say, dinner!"

Then addressing his valets, the King Snake yelled, "Bring him -- we shall dine later. But it gets long in hours this day, and I fear we have more to go. I am fearful of darkness, for when that happens, we shall be helpless and the gold lost!"

Chapter 8

Discovery!

Turnipseed and the king were nearing the meadow and flying about 50 feet above ground, dodging all the hardwoods and pines as they flew along the creek skirting the meadow. Turnipseed squeezed her knees together and Barty stopped short and hovered in the ground. There was little up and down movement by Barty, rather he stood almost motionless in the air.

"What?" The king asked.

"Below in the meadow -- can you see two lines moving?"

"I see grass moving -- almost like a line in the meadow-- there, to the west toward t he cornfield."

"That is so! Now look, over there, not 100 yards..."

"Another line -- much shorter than the first, however! Which means -- or at least I assume it means, that we have our people in the long line. Who do you think is the other line?"

"I don't know, but I have a hunch!" said Turnipseed. As she spoke, she spied Lodi approaching fast. Lodi had seen them, and was panicked.

"Lars! Turnipseed! The snake has Brimble -- they're trying to get Brimble to lead them to the Cauldron, but Brimble is in bad shape!" The words tumbled from her and she spoke almost without taking a breath. "It's my fault -- I accept blame. But I didn't think they would harm Brimble -- I just was making a deal to get a little more gold to furnish my little home!"

"You promised you wouldn't steal, Lodi," the king said, sternly. That was part of your penance!"

"Well," she said, "stealing is such a harsh word. We were just to take a small amount, but the Snake wants more -- in fact, he will kill Brimble if he doesn't get it all."

"Words of a snake!" Turnipseed said, "never trust the words of a Snake!"

"Be that as it may," said the King. "Right now is not the time to kill the Snake -- right now is the time to rescue Brimble! But he's been exposed to the daylight for some time. I worry that even without punishment from the Snake that he could very well die from exposure to the heat! "He looked Lodi squarely in the eyes. "What shape was he when you last saw him?"

"Not well, though coming off a stupor of a drunk! I left Addie to watch him, but I worry about Addie!"

"Lars -- look!" Turnipseed pointed to the small line moving through the grass. "It looks like the faeries are going to reach the cornfield before the Snake's column. What roads are in the corn?"

"There is a faint road close to where the Snake will come out...it isn't used much, but it's still pretty well defined...Why?"

"What if we were to remake the road by taking our column and give the snake a chance to be a big Wheel? What we do is have all the little people redesign a road in the cornfield that is very close to being correct, but is really going to take them in a big circle!"

"How will that save Brimble?"

"It will buy us time till darkness...You go and get the column moving spit-speed to the corn. Have Lodi give you directions from above and just swing the road in a soft circle and head it back to the meadows. The Snakes will have no idea that they are just heading back to where they started. I will go invisibly into the Snake's column and keep Brimble alive. You ride Barty. Lodi and I will fly!"

"I'll fall off, " said the King."

"No you won't. Barty is fantastic!"

Brimble was lying on a stretcher. His eyes were blackened, not from any physical abuse, but from the tremendous heat that he was suffering through. The Snake King had decided that a dead Brimble was of no use, because they could not find the gold any other way than through Brimble's help. But even taking a stretcher, Brimble was losing his consciousness to heat stroke.

Suddenly he smelled a waft of fruit and walnuts -- and it took a moment to register on his slowing brain. "Coo --", he said. "Turnipseed, HA, HA, HA! " And for the first time since last night, he felt there was hope.

The Snake was beside him in a moment. "I smell something very different -- fruity, walnuty, and with a smidgeon of Pecan!" He faced Brimble and Addie, who was being held close to Brimble. "Why do I smell fruitiness and walnutiness?"

"Well, it certainly isn't your breath," said Brimble, trying to smile. "Why is that so important to you? Are you afraid of being attacked by an apple? Or a walnut?" It hurt him to laugh, his lungs were congested, and he had coughed so much that his chest hurt. But he laughed a hearty laugh, pain or no pain and enjoyed the first real merriment that day!

The Snake spoke nothing, but slid past Brimble and Addie and hissed to Addie as he passed, "Helloo Addie -- I'm still looking forward-- to, shall we say, having you over for dinner tonight. With relish. Or drawn butter!" His laugh was long and sibilant.

Brimble stared at Addie. "If I didn't know better, Addie. He sounds like what's for dinner is YOU! Coo! Now isn't that freaky!"

"Turnipseed -- how am I supposed to signal the king? Are you picking my thoughts up? Perhaps you'd better join him down there" thought Lodi. "But then, how will I know even then, cause I can't hear your thoughts."

When the faerie king appeared to the column, the wanted reaction was to cheer, but the Snake's group was entirely too close for a full-out little people's yell, so in propriety, they basically did nothing loud.

"My fellow fairies -- we know where Brimble is and why he is not here with us right now. We have every reason to believe his is still alive and we are going to do everything in our power to save him. Right now, we believe him to be only about one mile to our due north on a south east track across the meadows heading directly on an oblique intersectional tangent to the new cornfield! He is being held by the Snake King – and they have an expedition!" The king brought in those closest to him, including the Sergeant and MorningStar. "Actually, Turnipseed is there right now to ascertain that he is going to make it. It is up to us to stop the Snake and his creatures from their evil deed anticipated to steal our gold from the Caldron that Brimble and Skinny Kenneth guard each and every night.

Lodi from above watched as Turnipseed launched like a rocket into the shallow heights and then dipped toward the faery king and the fairies. Lodi Repeated, "Give me visual assurance that you can hear me, Turnipseed." And she watched as Turnipseed produced a pyrotechnic burst in answer to her plea, then disappear under the grass.

Her greetings to the people of Faerieland were pithy and abrupt. "Ok, Lars, Ok fellow faeries and enchanted creatures. We are going to create a new Little People's road so when the Snake's columns hit the cornfield, they are going to follow a five minute old new road that we are going to make. But they won't realize is that it is a very slow curve that will bring them right to where they started from -- and it will take most of the rest of daylight to do so. By then, it being dark and all, they won't have a clue what has happened. That's when we make our boldest move to rescue Brimble."

Below her, Lodi saw the grass movement to the south begin to edge gently toward the north and east. "Turnipseed! I am running a mental tangent from the Snake's column to where it meets at the edge of the cornfield...and if you will drift about 10 or 15 degrees more to port, and then run straight -- it looks like about /18 mile, then run starboard about 7 degrees, and you should hit the mark for the Snake's roadway..." As she watched, the tiny movement in the grass turned almost exactly the 15 degrees and started forward.

Turnipseed was no good with all the figures, for she did know them, but lacked the time to really be thrilled by the reality of it all that good navigational figures gave. But MorningStar was there. MorningStar who was raised with the sextant was there.

Lodi watched as her directions were translated and turned in to action. First, the 15 degree port turn, then the starboard turn, then a slight more port adjustment. She made sure the paths did not cross prior to the corn for the smells and scents and other signs would certainly cause the wily Snake to lose faith in the cornfield run.

Turnipseed now had Barty back and on his well traveled back, she floated to the king, who stood in front with MorningStar. "I believe, your royalness, that Barty, Yourself and Me -- with

MorningStar to help define the trajectory of our new road, should perhaps have the first go at creating this new national treasure of a superhighway."

"I defer to you, your highness Turnipseed. I think it far more important for me to stay here and watch our flanks till all are all safely past'd. I shall bring up the rear, and we shall have safety between thee and me. He walked to her where she was seated on Barty and putting his arms around her, kissed her on the cheek.

"Do that again, Lars, and the Snake King will know I'm here just because of the blush." thought Turnipseed. Of course, Kings being all they are, probably never are even interested in whether their kiss would cause a blush. But of a King kissing a Faerie Queen, no one at all thought of looking for a blush. It would never have come into their mind for a second. But the king had something additional for Turnipseed. "I made a quick trip home and brought some things back for you. There's something in the bag that I want you to be sparing about, but use to our advantage. Back up this road a hundred feet or so and start dropping little amounts along the trail. We won't have a Snake King who's going to question this every time he licks the air. She opened the bag he gave her to peek in and smiled. It was full of chopped nuts, apples and bananas.

It was a twenty minute dash with every step guided by Lodi, and it had to be rapid because the road had to be built and had to be back to the starting point and then retreated to the other road, with passageways blocking the retreat after the retreat was made so there was no chance of the Snake's column's mistakenly taking the retreat instead of the new road.

Lodi watched breathlessly lest the Snake's column discover the Little People. "Turnipseed, you have about three or four minutes to finish your escape! The Snake King is by the cornfield and I can see grass moving from your stragglers!"

"Everybody! Don't say a word -- don't move a muscle -- Freeze!" They could hear noises now, no more than twenty or thirty feet away. They froze, because they could hear the Snake King himself! Turnipseed motioned to all to follow her example.

The Snake King once again had brought everybody to a halt. "There it is again -- that funny smell of fruit and nuts! He slithered back again to Brimble. "I've a good thought to just take you into the sun and leave you there, Brimble, let you ripen, as we shall say. I'd give you ten seconds to fully ripen in the direct sun!" He motioned to the stretcher bearers, "Put him down. I think he knows something about this smell -- the scent I smell is fruit and nuts -- and I want to know where it's coming from!"

Brimble propped himself up his elbows and drew in several strong whiffs. Almost it smelled still like Turnipseed, but this time, there was something more -- too much of a good things, as it were. He could catch the nuance of Turnipseed. Definitely. But he looked upon the ground and caught sight of some crumbles upon the pathway which he reached out his long, lanky arm and picked up a little fistful. "Something's happening," he thought. "An' I like the thought -- for some reason, this here's fresh apples and walnuts and pears -- they're tryin' to cover up old Turnipseed, they are!" With that he burst laughing. "You old prune," he called the Snake. Here's your source of all that fruity smell you smell. I had almost forgot, you old sot! It's the blessings of roads they do each year by spreadin' o' the apples and nuts upon the roads used by the little one's as they gather in their bounty for the next cold season. You being cold blooded an all wouldn't had no knowledge of it, I'm sure, because ye don't take na time to save and store for the cold season, cause ya'll be in hibernation. But the stores of nuts and fruits and dried fish and meats, why we look forward to winter for the plenty it brings because we've saved for it."

He patted Addie's little head, "Even Addie, cold blooded though he is, they put him in a room so cheery warm with a great fire, lots to drink and eat and a gentle friend to share his time with, and I dare say, Addie's ne'er hibernated a day in his life!"

Brimble felt a warm, wet kiss, and a voice in his ear. "Keep up the Blarney -- be as loud as you can. We've re-built the road. You're going to go in circles. At least you will till it starts to darken. Eat the apple I left in your pocket. And we'll be back to get you in evening tide."

"Thank you Turnipseed. Save Addie, too!"

Chapter 9

Promises to keep!

Although Snakes by nature are cunning and conniving, as remembranced from our first Mother and her experience with them, they are decidedly not very smart in analyzing the facts at hand. You and I would probably question finding nuts and fruits on our highways in a very different manner than did the Snake King, but we forgive his stupidness because he did not want any conclusions that would cause him to place anything in the way of his pursuit of the task at hand. So any question that could be simplistically answered could be cast aside to not interfere with the quest for the Caldron.

The final members of the Little Folk's expedition backed graciously down the spur they had built to intersect with the Snake King's column, and as best they could, they tried to return it to original meadow. The Snake King was not suspicious because he had no reason to be so. Rather, he quickly leaped from the meadow to the road that ran into the cornfield and the column quickly followed.

"I love a road like this -- because it is so true, so easy to follow," Snakey told the Lizard King. This will teach those faeries to mess with real things like we snakes and lizards. Because we are getting close to their money. I can almost feel it!" He paused a moment to reflect, "But I don't like the set that the sun is taking, for the very sky is not as bright as it were just a few moments ago! We must press on."

"What if we don't make it before sundown," asked the Lizard King. "What happens when Brimble get's his powers back?"

"Bah!" said the Snake. "You worry too much, Lizard. Brimble is so weak now, it will take him a week to recover from what he has now. How now that he would get all his powers back in just a few minutes or hours tonight? Let us be positive, it will not happen."

A few feet away, Brimble and Addie were carrying on a most surreptitious conversation.

"Brimble. Turnipseed loosed my bonds when she was here last, but told me not to leave you. I would not, anyway. I will stay with you until the snake tries to have me for dinner tonight!"

"As in try to eat you for dinner?"

"That is his plan."

"Oh! That is what he meant when he said that he was having you for dinner. He is having you for dinner!"

"So he thinks. I'll leave before then, surely. But Turnipseed left this plan. We're in a circle here--"

Brimble cut in.. "Turnipseed tried to tell me, but I couldn't understand her".

"When it is dark, "Addie continued, "they will notice that they are not making progress and they will stop for the night. They're not going to worry about you, because magic or not, you're not going to be a factor because it will take several days for you to recuperate, darkness or not. They'll post guards, but they're not going to look for your help to come straight from above. The king and Skinny are going to lift you to the clouds tonight! I'll be here to tie you on."

Brimble looked at the earnest froggy, and more like a sneeze that you try to contain than a hearty laugh, Brimble managed to sound like both with a big guffaw! The King slowed only momentarily and turning to the lizard, he said, "That is why we will always be so far above them in every way. Because they are so simply stupid!" He moved on, engulfed in warm, self-congratulations.

Something was wrong. For over an hour, the group had blitzkreiged across the cornfield, absolutely certain that they would now find their utopia on the other side, a short walk to the caldron, and then a night of celebration before returning with all the gold they could transport in bags and stretchers. But now they had the terrible revelation that they had been here before. And being in tall meadow growth, with the sun becoming dimmer and dimmer, they had no way to reconnoiter to find out where they were. "I say, let's just not jump to nerves," said the Lizard King. "We can clear out a small place, find some dry fodder and have us a comfy little fire, have some rose-hip tea and enjoy night's sleep. The faeries aren't going to find us tonight

It was agreed. Soon, little tents were strung from cornstalk to cornstalk. Little enclaves of troops were warming hands, roasting baby cattails and drinking from large steins great gallons of fine apple juices and ciders. Above them, as the darkness deepened, Lars and Lodi and Skinny Kenneth and Turnipseed and Barty were starting to assemble on a few little tumbling fluffy clouds. Even the moon was beginning to show.

Below them in the cornfields, they could see several little warm yellowish-red campsites glowing up through the night air. Lars gave Skinny Kenneth a coil of rope.

"Say, Guv," said Kenneth, "but I don't reckon there's enough rope here -- maybe only half of what we need."

"Not so, Kenneth. You see only what you must see. Lay your hand atop the pile again, laddie!" said he. Kenneth reached over and rested his hand on the pile. He could feel it, grasp it, and yet his hand lay atop the rope pile a good three feet above it. The King continued. "They will not see the rope that has come for Brimble. Turnipseed and Lodi will tie about Brimble's waist with the rope you cannot see, and then you shall begin to pull him up. I shall let you know when, and ye shall then heave ho smartly, Kenny, and ye shall have saved the day!"

"Coo!", Kenny said. Everyone loves to have saved the day, and now it was his turn. Frankly, the Leprechauns, having to rely on other than a lot of magic, were by far the best physical specimens of all of faeriedom, and that took into account all of their drinking and chasing about. Kenneth was no exception.

Walnuts and Fruits. The scent brought Brimble back to consciousness from a light sleep. The entire camp was quiet, fierce warriors lay in little sleeping rolls about the fires. Their frightening helmets garishly outfitted with tiny goat horns had tenderly been placed close to their pillows and now little teddy bears were clutched beneath the covers, and the soft suckling sound each made as the suckled on blankie corners or thumbs lulled all to deep sleep. The fires were banked, and slowly began to lose all light and heat.

Brimble felt the course hemp rope already tied about his waist. It was cinched hard so there was no fear of his slipping the bonds between earth and heaven. Turnipseed whispered into his ear. "We are having Kenneth rescue you, lad. You are not strong enough to survive my invisibility -- so this shall be a dangerous ordeal. But we are there to shore your courage up!"

The Snake King woke quickly from his sleep. He listened to Brimble, but could not determine who he was talking to. Addie was not there. The Snake had teased Addie, but had no intentions of devouring the frog, because there would probably be another time that he would need Lodi. Yet, he was glad Addie had somehow escaped, because the more he thought about that tasty little morsel, why yes, his resolve was weakening and he could indeed have had Addie for dinner, after all. Who could have blamed him? It was the nature of the beast, after all.

But he was not about to let Brimble escape! Because without Brimble, where was the gold?

So he left his soft pile of silk pillows and slithered past his sleeping guards, ("who is protecting whom?" he had asked, as he slipped past them. He let his tail tip rub a little under the nose of one guard, who reached to scratch, then snorted, then giggled, then said "mama!" and was soon snoring deeply again) and sidled up to Brimble. Everything looked alright, except that Brimble was feigning sleep.

That was not right. It was, after all, Brimble's daybreak. When he came awake.

"Ah, Brimble my friend. I don't know who you are talking with. But you are up to something. And I need to know. So, let us become more inseparable, you and I!" Brimble watched through slit eyes, still pretending to take big deep sleeping breaths.

He watched as the Snake king coiled his last small length into a knot about one of Brimble's legs. It was tenuous at best, but would probably temporarily keep the Snake connected to Brimble. Brimble suppressed a chuckle as he wondered how long the king could hold on for a vertical getaway -- which is something the Snake King had no inclination of.

At the moment no more sunset existed, King Lars simply said, "Now" to Kenneth, and Skinny Kenny began the arm over arm lifting of Brimble. There was not resistance, for Brimble had wasted to little weight. At the other end of the rope, Brimble felt himself begin to jerk into the air. The progress started smooth and quick, but once Skinny Kenneth realized the amount of time he would endure pulling up, the routine settled into a distinct five yard hike, a pause to replace his hands and again the pull. But there was more than Brimble on the line.

The Snake awoke with a snort! And he Shouted, "Awake, camp, awake! They are stealing Brimble." Brimble, in his weakened state, replied, "You're snakiness honor! They are also stealing you."

"I shall untie myself, and the guards will be right here. It is only a disconvenience."

"Really, sire? I should take another look before I untied myself, were I you!"

The king looked about. This was -- different. "Bring a lantern -- quickly. "

"Yes sire -- to where shall I bring it?"

He saw the lantern. But was it to the left of him? Or to the right of him? It did not look right to him. Nor did it seem right to him his own positioning. For honestly, the lantern appeared to be directly below him! He looked above him. Brimble seemed to be suspended in air. Yet every few moments, he would see Brimble jerk another few feet -- and it was toward the stars!

"Sire!" The sentry with the lantern called out. "I am right BELOW you. You are only about twenty-five feet up or so -- so let go. You snakes can withstand that kind of a fall! But you're going up at about five feet or so every move! "

"I'm not going to let go! We're not going to lose our gold, " yelled the Snake King. The faeries are not killers...they're not going to kill me..."

"Letting you die is another thing entirely, "yelled up the sentinel.

"Now is not the time for semantics, " yelled down the snake. Let us not argue -- wake everybody! I need help!"

"I'll say you do, your slimy highness," Brimble thought. "Turnipseed, we have an unwelcome guest -- we don't need to let him die, but if he don't get off soon, he's gonna die when he finally lets go!"

"Addie -- get down there, leave Lodi here. "Turnipseed said. "This might be a way for you to help out -- The King Snake has tied himself about Brimble. We don't want to kill him -- but if he doesn't let loose soon, he's going to kill himself. We'll stop here for awhile."

"How nice to see you again, your Snakiness, " said Addie, and pulled just outside of the kings swinging lunge to hover.

"That is a bad situation you seem to be in. By-the-by, sorry, but I had other plans tonight, so I could not join you for Dinner."

"I am so glad you had the chance to leave -- you would have been lovely for dinner, but then I couldn't have had you here to help me, either, so it certainly is working out for the better, I should say, Addie!" "On the other hand," the Snake thought, "having a good frog dinner is certainly better than getting nothing out of the whole day. And with that, he began to swing back and forth, back and forth, like some giant pendulum, gently increasing the arc with each swing.

Addie eyes were shut as if he contemplated how to help the king without being eaten.

What he was really doing was timing the arcs. He knew what the King intended. The king drew near on the next one.

Brimble was in communication with Turnipseed. "On the next swing, when I say 'Go', have Kenny drop the line three feet. That ought to do it. He had felt the knot of the snake's body soften, and knew that the snake was about to let go"

The swing started, the final grip was ready to open by the snake. Brimble said aloud and in thought, "Go!" The entire line dropped, and the Snake let go his grip and opened his mouth to receive Addie. Instead he saw Addie suddenly sitting motionless, hanging in air above him, and he felt himself in a perfect Royal one-and-a-half gainer dive, skewer a cornstalk as if he were a projectile from a Snake gun" and with his speed cut in half because of the cornstalk intrusion , he hit the ground with a thud!

"You're safe!" yelled the sentinel to the King. "But I know I've left half my ribs back there", the Snake King moaned, as he straightened himself out and began to crawl back to the group. "Now how do we get our fair share of the gold?"

"Perhaps it's not ours," said the sentinel. "Glad you're not hurt, Sire!"

"Shaddap!" said the Snake King in reply.

Addie rejoined Lodi and the King and all the rest above. Lodi and Addie were still in their smaller state, and Lodi snuck aboard Addie. "Go," she whispered. The king didn't even turn about to watch, but said as they were leaving. "We need to talk about this, Lodi! Soon!"

And that is how Turnipseed helped Lars save all the money for Faierieland. And why there are still coins available everyday for the millions of boys and girls who have Turnipseed change their baby teeth for shiny new coins. How else? How else indeed!"

Postlogue

Three days after the fiasco, and definitely after dark, the King, smartly dressed with a new suite with long legs and beautiful silken waistcoat, entered the little hospital with Turnipseed at his side. Though the King was fit and cut a beautiful figure with his whitened silk, Turnipseed's light royal blue of crushed silk satins shone as a cut emerald on the white gold background flashed with the rarest of natural beauty, doubly so by the fact that Lars did not try any kind of a one-upmanship but let Turnipseed's beauty broadcast itself. There was no cranny or shadow not filled with the beauty of Turnipseed.

By the time they had climbed the rounded stairway to the second floor, all in the hospital knew true Royalty was in the building. As they walked along, the read the chart names posted on each door, moving along until they came to one door identified as S. King, His Honor. At the door, the two posted standard bearers bowed low to Lars and Turnipseed, who more than returned the curtsey.

The Snake King lay upon his hospital bed, fully encased in a body-length cast. He had been in the dumps for most of two days, but as these two lovelies asked his leave to join him was a great honor, and his solemn countenance lit as the brightest candle and the room nearly swam in the great warmth of his genuine happiness to see them.

"This is so wonderful of you two to come visit, "the snake king enthused. Lars and Turnipseed went to the bed together and each gave the Snake King a cheek kiss and patted his cast before laying their flowers upon the small table.

"I'll have the nurse arrange this in a vase...it's so nice of you to bring flowers!"

Lars motioned at the cast. "What happened?"

Snake King replied, "Haven't you heard? I had a nasty spill a few days ago -- broke a few ribs. But I'll be alright. Nice of you to ask...King Lars!"

And then, he turned to Turnipseed. "Of course, this is such a pleasure to actually meet you, Turnipseed. I have heard so much about you through the years. But I never anticipated that I would ever get to meet you! " He looked quizzically at her. There is something different about you, though." He stopped and sniffed the air. "Walnuts! Fruit!" His eyes grew big, like large bagels with pupils where the holes would be. He started to cry, "Nurse!" and with that he started to choke.

"Nurse!"

Lars grabbed Turnipseed's hand and pulled her toward the door. "We really must take our leave, sir. I am sorry we have upset you with our presence." The Snake King did not respond except to continue to yell for the nurse. Once at the door, Lars glanced over his shoulder, then with a scolding smile, back at Turnipseed.

"You really shouldn't have worn that perfume. It's nighttime, you don't have an odor to worry about. But you wore that perfume! You shouldn't have!"

Turnipseed stole a glance at the snake and then looked deeply into Law's eyes. "Indubitably I should have!" And they walked into the dark from the hospital.

Chapter 11

Freddie and Tommy join the Army!

This little story is dedicated to Rebecca's children.

Brimble and Skinny Kenneth really had very little to do during the night, for humans, being humans, could never find the rainbows end with the pot of gold coins! None could fault them; for trying, however, since they did spend an inordinate amount of time looking for it. In fact, if they had put the energy they spent trying to get rich for nothing into hard work, it is conceivable they would have made as much money as was in t he cauldron in the first place. Oh, perhaps not so. But they would have made more money than they ever did trying to find the pot of gold.

Especially so if you will remember that the rainbow end with the gold was the nighttime rainbow that most humans cannot see, anyway!

So the two elves mainly would sit in front of the GE model 70 color television with the eight inch screen and watch television. Being only about two feet high themselves, that was indeed a wide screen. And they would either drink root beer floats made with Elfin root beer or leave out the ice cream and just drink bitter ale. Then, morningtime, they would zip away to their homes as fast as you can say stomach ache!

Being Leprechauns, they never gained any weight, and really were extremely satisfied with their existence.

And every night a knock or two would come at the door, and in would come Freddie and Tommy and share a pint or two before they would go back into the night and get serious about finding something to eat.

But tonight something was, well, in the air with the two. Skinny Freddie immediately could sense it. "What are you two up to tonight?" he said, and opened the door without an invitation, because he knew they would be right in.

Freddie took his bulk to the love seat that Skinny Freddie had just left, and brushing it off with two of his hairy legs, plumped his rather large bottom straightway upon it. Tommy followed and sat beside Tommy.

Of course they accept the pints and blowing the top off, they drink with different speeds. No one said anything, yet the two leprechauns kept looking expectantly at the two. After a minute or two of non-discourse, they all looked together at the television. Finally Tommy broke the silence.

"Tommy and me has decided to join King Lar's army. We think he's a great chap is a king what we would fight for."

Freddie hoisted his partially filled mug and raised a toast. "Here, Here!"

"Anyway, to continue in the same vein," Freddie went on, "we have gained a rather deserved reputation as to being fearsome in our endeavors. Endeavors such as guardin' the pot for you, and keeping certain undesirables such as stink bugs out of the cave where the Gold is."

To that, Tommy felt it his absolute requirement to butt-in. "May I say we do not do it for food, nay, forbid it, because nothing is as foul smelling as a stink bug, and that is certainly no tasty treat..."

With that, Skinny Kenny sat down his drink upon the coffee table. It was, he felt, time to make a good point that these two would understand.

"I know how you pine to participate, surely, " he said. (Yet there was no way he knew how they pined to join the army, since he had never had -- nor would he ever have -- any desire to join a regimented group such as the King's army.) But have you thought this over? You know, you two are never the most welcome guest at a party..."

"How would we know," bespoke Tommy. "After all, hardly anyone's ever invited us to one, I recollect."

"He's right, you know. Both of you. Certainly you're both right." Freddie added this as he looked idly into his drink.

"Thank you for letting me continue, "Skinny Freddie said, not without a certain tone of superiority in his voice. "That's just what I was going to get at if you would let me continue..."

"The floor's yours, "said Freddie in an extremely non-conciliatory tone.

"I don't want to hurt you gen'lmen, but how will you even march in the army when nobody really --ah, I don't want to say this wrong, cause I don't want to hurt you..." Again, he trailed off for he could not phrase the thought without hurting his friends. "But let's face it, no one's gonna want to march with you because won't everyone just be thinking that you're looking for dinner?" He paused and shook his head slowly. "Scary thought...scary thought."

Freddie was known to go half-cocked with a little temper. And he was steamed. "Have we had you two for dinner yet? By gosh, no! We deserve a chance! "He calmed some, and continued.

"You know, we come with natural weapons -- why my kind are world-renown for jumpin!..."

"It ain't the Olympics, Freddie, "Brimble said, and laughed. "I don't mean to hurt you none, but how is jumping such a great thing?"

"We jump and eat birds!"

"Have you ever, " Brimble asked.

"No, I haven't.   But I have read about it in your Encyclopedia. We are venomous and we can attack birds and all other kinds of creatures. Even the Big people are afraid of us."

"That's because we are rather ugly," Tommy said. "You have to admit that!"

"I don't think you and I are ugly at all. We're both extremely good looking for our species!" Freddie said, defending both he and Tommy.

Skinny Kenny and Brimble exchanged glances, sat for just a few seconds, and in an immediate face-about, chuckled, drank their drink and put their attention back to the TV. Brimble was occupied for only a few minutes before turning back.

"Then do it! You need a letter from us? You'll get one."

"I don't think so, I really don't think we need a letter, "Freddie said as he too went back to his drink. "We're already good friends with the king and Princess Turnipseed. We shall travel tonight and call on them on the morrow's eve!"

"Well, here's to you -- both! Godspeed," said Skinny Kenny and with that he chugged at his mug till the amber liquid with it's thick head had slid down the mug and was gone.

Chapter 12

Freddie and Tommy Enlist

This time the knock on the door was definitely different. Rather than a solid 'Knock - Knock', it was almost in staccato. Such as a "knock-knock-knock-knock" with little case letter 'k's' -- and not upper case as in the solid 'Knock-Knock'.

Turnipseed was tired this morning, more so than usual. For some reason the number of deciduous teeth that had been lost was greater than any night she could ever remember. And though in her nightly rounds time stood still and she moved millions of times in just seconds -- and even though all this was done in just one night (for tomorrow there would certainly be millions of more teeth to change for shiny coins) -- when the volume was so great as it had been this night, it did make her very tired. In fact, she did not even turn on the telly for the insipid shows that she could feel chagrinned about. She just had enjoyed a dainty cup of exquisite chocolate prior to bed when the tremulous little knocking came to her door.

In spite of this, she walked with some reserved joyousness toward the door. After all, who but King Lars himself had the chutzpa to call on her in the early morning. Surely none of the rest of the little people would do such a thing and disturb her sleep..

"I'm coming, Lars, "she said and without bothering for any thought transfer, she slightly opened the door at first. After all, what if it were not Lars?

With a calmness acquired after years of never finding things as they should be, but only as they really are, she looked rather warily at the two visitors outside her door.

The spider spoke first to quell any apprehension. "You don't need to worry, your Princessness. We are not here to eat you."

"We certainly are not," added the scorpion. "Do you remember us, your highness? I'm Tommy and this is Freddie? He's a tarantula. I'm a scorpion."

"How could I forget you two? Weren't you about to eat the king at one time?"

"No, we weren't really going to eat him. We would have found out he was king, I'm sure. Yes, I'm positive we would have. There is something different about kings, and I'm certain we wouldn't have eaten him -- because he is king, and the Great Creator protects kings, I have heard. That certainly is more than I can do!"

Turnipseed stood taken aback. She was not certain what was going on. She was also not certain what she had just heard from the mouth of the spider. She tried to say something, but the words stuck in her throat.

Freddie spoke again. "I am certain this is difficult for you to understand, because I don't always make that much sense when I talk. You understand of course that we mainly read. We don't talk much, certainly not in the day, but we do enjoy some good debates with the leprechauns at night when they're there. But mostly we read -- old Geographics, that sort of thing."

Tommy struck in. "But then, we don't have to make much sense -- because you can read our minds, anyway."

Turnipseed said to herself, "I'm not sure they have a mind -- I can't pick up a thing but funny sounds!" Then aloud, she said, with a lilting laugh, "No, really I can't yet -- I'm afraid you must think in your native tongues." She hesitated momentarily, then remembered that Fairy Queens are always adequately proper for any occasions.

"I have forgot my manners -- won't you please come in!"

Once inside, they sat upon the sofa -- the gold brocade sofa with hand-crocheted doilies covering the back and smaller matching doilies on the arm rests. Turnipseed disappeared into the kitchen, calling back to the two visitors that she was going to make tea and asked them how they liked their tea. Once inside the kitchen, she went to the little room that led off from the kitchen and opening it, called quietly to Addie:

"Stay there, stout heart. I have visitors out here that you are uncomfortable with. Anyway, the spider and scorpion are here. I don't believe they plan on eating anyone, leastwise Faeries. So you stay here and do not be tempting to them, you rapscallion piglet!"

On short notice, she brought out a plate of cold roast beef and some thickly sliced bread that she had made herself. Her platter also held cheeses and olives and pickles, which the two travelers loaded onto small plates she had brought out while she poured them each a hot mug of chamomile tea thickened with cream and honey.

The she sat upon her small rocker and tucked an Afghan about her body. "Now what brings you two so many miles from your -- abodes." What a satisfactory, non-pejorative word! Abode!

"We have come to be your champions and to serve the king!" Freddie said, with a large bravado! Tommy raised his hand in salute! "You and the King!" he fairly shouted. "God save you and the King!"

"I hope he shall-- save me from you and he," thought Turnipseed. "Thank you for the kind words," she said aloud. "That is wonderful! My champions! You and he!"

"That's right," said Freddie. "Me and he!" Tommy said quietly, nearly reverently," We come to join the King's army. Can you help us?"

Suddenly kind intentions and thoughts -- not in words, but deeply felt emotions and good will swirled into Turnipseed's mind -- Freddie's thoughts -- Tommy's thoughts. Never again would she have fear of these two gentle creatures -- fully intent on just the right to serve the right.

She looked at them, and her heart softened with their goodness. "I have it on good authority that the king indeed does listen to me -- now eat hearty, my new found friends. Eat hearty!" It was not long before the plates were wiped clean, and mugs drained. As the mellow light from the window swept across the room that day, two soldiers to be slept away, covered by the Faerie Princess' two best quilts, daintily quilted by Mrs. Sergeant Mouse and her many friends as gifts to Turnipseed.

Addie had awakened from his sleep and come into the room. He looked about at the fairy queen asleep in her rocker and the two guests on the sofas. There was nothing fearful any longer in the room. He returned to his room and fell asleep.

Chapter 13

King Lars again!

It was evening again and time to set off to meet King Lars. But Turnipseed made certain they would not go away hungry. Just in case. After a big breakfast of kippered herring, sour cream and eggs and waffles drenched in raspberry syrup, washed down with glass after glass of cold milk, their bellies could almost drag the floor with fullness.

When they had finished, Freddie wiped his mouth with one of the handy arms and asked, "Was that bacon", (realize of course that bacon is not on the everyday menu consumed by spiders and scorpions -- in fact, they had never had what we consider a proper breakfast. Usually their breakfast consisted of a bug or another, less-related spider or scorpion.)

"Certainly not, Freddie. Bacon is a rather delicious accoutrement made from the smoked underbelly of a pig -- (and nodding toward Addie, who dozed by the fireplace) and it, for obvious reasons, is never eaten in this house!"

"I beg your pardon -- I did not know. What did we have that was so delicious?"

"Kippers -- smoked herring, if you will."

"Oh yes," Freddie said. "Fish -- I have seen them in Skinny Kenny's National Geographic. They are a salt water, i.e., ocean fish, caught primarily in the North Atlantic and northern seas. Very good...."

"You read?" asked Turnipseed asked incredulously.

Tommy interjected, "his problem is that he reads too much -- now he isn't satisfied until he's seen what he reads about!"

"Amazing." Ejaculated Turnipseed. "Indeed?"

Freddie spoke again. "Shall we have kippers each morning in the army.

Turnipseed looked first at Addie before she spoke. "No. You'll probably have bacon and eggs."

-In the old days, long before Lars was born, back in the old country, faerie kings lived an opulent, almost unbelievable life, waited hand and foot upon by a large staff of faerie servants and enchanted animals, as such as the hedgehog and other English countryside animals. The royal family wore the richest fabrics of silks and satins and wonderful brocades that took hundreds of faerie women months to produce. And -- sad as it to relate, the royal family took advantage of their station for they placed heavy burdens upon the faeries and the gnomes both in servitude and taxation. That is why prince Pythany and his sweet cousin, Princess Gwendylyn disappeared, for they did not wish to see their friends in continual servitude required of them by Pythany's parents, King Rodney and Queen Pruscilla. Nearly half of the faerie land disappeared the day that Pythany and Gwendylyn disappeared -- but it was not coincidental that within the next several years, a whole colony of faeries and trolls and elves and Leprechauns were seen by a special few in the meadows and bogs of Maryland and Pennsylvania, and -- aye-- even in some of the Southern areas below Maryland.

Lars was their grandson -- and he inherited or was taught by nature to be good-natured, kind and outright goodly in his reign. He was usually known as Lars, not King or King Lars. In stature, he was not particularly tall nor was he particularly well-muscled. But he was average height for a faerie and average build, which is slighter than the Big People. He was someone that everyone wanted as their friend, and occasionally, if the times suited it, their king.

Right now, the kingdom needed a king, not a friend. And Lars felt himself aloof from some of his subjects who wished it that way. For it meant something to have a king all would respect and look upwards to. So during those times, he become "y'r Majesty". And though he dressed in clothes reminiscent of the mid-1700's, he was not treated as the boy next door, but as the genuine article -- his majesty the King.

He sat by himself in the Fairbucket Meadow at a table quite close to the door to the kitchen. He too was having kippers and eggs. The thought of bacon, after having the whole kingdom saved in part by a flying miniature pig, was unappetizing at the least. And he was having the most odd thought this morning, for visions of scorpions and spiders kept leaping about in his mind. And the narrator to this disturbing scene seemed to be the voice of Turnipseed! How absurd!

Presently bodies came flying by him rushing to escape by the back door. In this late night of evening, between day and the light of the orange-colored lanterns, he saw two dark shadows block the light as the outside door swung wide. Then the smell hit him. The dark, damp smell of the cave.

Now he understood his thoughts. Turnipseed was warning him? Notifying him?

"There he is, your royal highness. I don't bet you remember us," And with that Freddie extended his hand. Well, one of his hands. Or perhaps it was a leg.

Their visage would remain etched in the King's mind. Tommy with a red bandana holding his underclothes and a change of socks hung like a lantern from his stinger so that the bag was only inches behind his head, and Freddie with his Barbie back pack held by two legs. It's contents continually rolled about since the pack was horizontal, not vertical.

The king held out his hand for the two ragamuffins, thought for a moment about hugging each, and quickly changed his mind. 'It is difficult to change the animal,' he thought to himself. But still, in his heart, he did feel an affection for these two. (Had he known how they would serve him in the future, the feeling of affection would have been greatly multiplied.) "Freddie! Tommy! What a pleasant sight it is to see you this evening! Of course I remember you -- guardians of the pot!"

Tommy spoke up. "That's us, your royalness. But that is not our choice today, for we have come a longsome way to offer ourselves as your cavaliers!"

"What he means, your honor, is that we crave excitement -- and the thrill of heated battle!" And then Freddie misquoted the poet, "Once again into the fray rode Freddie and Tommy -- to rescue their newfound king and his kingdom from his enemies!"

The king laughed, and then looking at Tommy's stern visage, immediately regretted his gaff!

"I was just going to say that our kingdom is not much in need of rescuing today, gentlemen"

Tommy's stern look softened and his mouth curled up into a smile. "Oh, but there is trouble at the gate, there is, there is, your honor! For we have overheard the creatures that steal both by night and morning that the Snake King is planning a retaliation for the embarrassment he suffered that you and her royal princess, the Turnipseed, wreaked in havoc amongst those that slither and crawl upon their bellies, the snakes and the lizards..."

"Even the great beasts the cats, though they can't keep much of a truce, with the cats always wanting the lizards for dinner." added Freddie. "They are terribly suspicious of each other, for certain. But Tommy tells it true, for we both heard some sentry's at a bonfire along the way. We watched from the dark in the grass so they wouldn't know we were on to them!"

The king, who had no reason to doubt them, was visibly troubled, for he stood and walked back and forth among the stools and tables of the pub. "Do you know what the little slitherer is up to? Did you hear what he was going to do? Or when?"

"No sir, we just heard them laughing. As you can imagine, without visible appendages for hearing as you have in them ears, why a lot of what was being said probably sailed right past us, for we have nothing to stop the sound."

The king stopped his pacing and looked directly at the speaker, Tommy. He thought, 'If there were ever a question that the insecticide world has very little brain -- if any, that would verify it.' But thinking further, he realized that what the scorpion said was true -- they had to be right next to the speaker to understand what the speakers were saying.

The king sat and eyed again his visitors. Certainly not, in looks, were these two material for his army, with it's beautiful uniforms and colorful hats and banners. These two were road weary, hoary with beards (yes, they both had considerable beards from the journey) caked with the dust of the march. Why did not Turnipseed offer them baths? The answer was clear, for a lady does not permit her overnight guests to bathe, especially these two, for who knew what instincts were imbedded deeply into their, shall we dare say? - brains. But. Would the Snake King or his captains ever believe these two were from their enemies and were spies? Never!

And that is how Freddie and Tommy joined the army that evening.

Chapter 14

Freddie and Tommy become spies!

Earnest Snifflesnout was just your average sand lizard. He had done well in high school -- but after that! He just drifted through along with no goals and no ambition. His parents had done everything to try to get him interested in Green Lizards University, but though he had the grades, and had been accepted, he frankly had little interest in attending school, and dropped out after his first semester!

Well, what do young lizards do who have no job, no interests, and no college education? His parents did what any smart parent does -- they forced him to join the Army! To get the discipline and self-awareness that donning a uniform in defense of one's homeland! What indeed had happened, however, was not what his parents wished (nor did they probably even know!) -- he had turned into a goldbrick! And a lazy one at that!

Today, because of his success in a secret activity for the king, he had only to pull guard duty for three hours, and then he was off again to go the pub and party!

He stood at semi-attention at the guard gate to the king's castle with his best friend, Hermie.

"Psst! Hermie -- over there -- someone's in the Shadows..." he whispered. He could see movement, but he had no idea that it was anything.

Hermie was bored. "It's just a rat or something, "

Earnie thought it over. That's what it must be. For sure. It moved again!

"I saw something move over there!"

He turned toward Hermie to point. As he did, he saw fear in Hermie's eyes. Hermie was pointing. "Look!"

As if by an enchantment, two creatures stood before the sentries. One was an enormous spider! The kind that they had only read about. Big enough to kill a bird! The other, a shiny black, gigantic horrible Scorpion. The scorpion carried a bandana on his stinger that Ernie could only guess at what gruesomeness the sack contained. A head of a lizard, perhaps! And the spider, with a knapsack that the spider continually adjusted with one of its legs...or arms, who knows which or what a spider would call their appendages, certainly not Ernie!

Freddie, always the first to speak in nearly any situation, spoke first this time. And to the small lizard, his breath was thick with the scent of decayed animals and insects! (Actually, it still smelled like the fish he had consumed that very morning not four hours past!).

"We are bandits from far off land! We kill anything that we don't reckon we have any other need for, and we eat them on the spot!"

Tommy dipped his bag slightly, "Arr! Arrr!" he growled in his most menacing manner.

Freddie continued, in a low voice that seemed to rumble inside his throat before it came out in a gravely sound like rocks make when you walk on them. "You!..."

"Me?" Hermie's voice, on the other hand, was weak, like a kitten's frightened meow."

"The king? You want to see the king? Have you any intention of eating the king? I should know now, you know, you see! Because I really would have to disarm you or stop you or something, you know? Because I can't have you eating our king tonight, really! It would sort of put me out of business as his guard, you see?" Hermie spoke a lot and quickly when he was frightened, and right now, his spear was trembling so hard that it fell from his desperate grasp with a clatter on the stone underneath his feet, and he continued babbling uncontrollably.

This time Tommy spoke first. "We don't want to eat your king -- we don't like snakes! At least not to eat 'em. In my recollection, they are rather little meat and a lot of ribs! We understand that the king can always use a few good men, though -- and we are two of the best!"

Actually, the king was looking for a few good – no men, certainly – but he knew that tarantulas and scorpions were mean and brazen. So he felt the word "good" was hardly a word to characterize these two creatures. He hoped fervently that they were actually not "good". But rather were instead the opposite and quite "bad."

Sliding along, he skinnied up one of the posts that held the canopy over the throne and then, as if grabbing the post with a hand (although we all know it was his tail, he pushed his head directly into the face of the giant spider.

"I understand you catch birds and eat them," he said with a large amount of sinister hissing.

"Actually, it's far more difficult than one would imagine to catch birds, you see. But then to ascribe to Newton, I don't imagine the weight of the spider would be enough…" Freddie paused and glanced at Tommy who was surreptitiously rolling his eyes, trying to get Freddie's attention. When he caught Freddie's gaze, he made a mean face, furrowing his brow lowly over his eyes and screwing his mouth into an exaggerated scowl.

Freddie looked back into the king's eyes. "Yeah, sure. All the time. Why, this morning, in fact, I had two sparrows and a blackbird for breakfast!" He paused while the Snake King continued to gaze and then breaking the stare, the snake wound his way further up the post;

"What say! I like you boy. And you too," he finished, glancing at Tommy. "I am so excited that I have not been able to sleep. Let me show you why.

Chapter 15

The Great Discovery

The King watching closely to make certain of their secrecy, especially to discern anyone following them through the dark of night, entered a room dug into the river bank through quite a large opening and with a wave of his tail, waived the little group of four others to join him in the room.

Not the snake hole one would suppose, for after all, the king was a snake, and the lizard king, was, as you might further guess, a lizard (what else?) And nearly all of their servants and warriors and whatnots were probably not over three or four inches high, the lot of them! So they didn't need a big entrance to anything. Except -- there it was! A hole in the riverbank that was at least, oh! nearly a foot wide.

The two beautifully carved pine doors were elaborate with decorations of the king and his warriors, the king and his great white miniature horse, the king and his trusted advisors-- well, you get the picture well enough! Earnie lay his spear aside and grasping the large pull-ring, tugged with great might to get the doors to move and they finally opened outward with a great groan at their hinges.

"Terrific doors", exulted Tommy! "Wonderful stuff!"

The snake spoke to order Earnie to keep vigil at the door and the two spies could hear the command echoing about what must surely be a large room. The king threw a switch and the light revealed a cavernous room with the yellow light of the flashlight bulb used for light casting sharp, black shadows all through the room. It casts dark cast-shadows where the cave diggers had not evened out the shovel marks from the excavation.

A huge shadow was cast upon the far wall by a giant form that filled the center of the room. It was covered with a canvas and stood nearly ten times the height of the tallest of the trio. However, considering that the tallest in the room was Freddie, and the object was nearly 12 inches off the ground, it was a monolith indeed. The blue tarp that covered the object was held down at the four corners by spikes. Yes the connecting corners were tight and stretched to the point they strained with every waft of air -- especially from the outside air as the door opened.

The King slid to the room's center to the edge of the tarp and slid under. He motioned with his tail for the other two to follow. There, above them in the air, literally hovering and straining at the blue tarp was a large, bulging, silvery cigar shaped sphere. Actually, it looked strangely like a heart -- and had red printing on the side. Could it be a UFO? A spaceship? Underneath, hanging from dozens of small ropes that disappeared over the top, was a picnic basket -- a small Easter-type woven of cane. It attached at the sides to all the ropes cascading down from the metallic-looking sphere. Ah, a true THING of BEAUTY!"

"Is that a space ship, your royalness?" asked Freddie, in a voice at once fairly wrung with disbelief at the apparition.

"It looks like one, doesn't it!" the king exclaimed with great relish. "And looks here," he added, pointing to the large red letters on the sphere's side.

Freddie spelled out the writing. "H - A - P - P - Y   B - I - R - T - H - D - A - Y"

The king looked at Freddie in complete wonderment. "You can spell?"

Freddie bristled at the wonderment of the King. "What do you take me for? A complete idiot?

Of course I can spell. I read a lot. Mostly old National Geographic, though, I have never seen the word birthday, I can take the root words of 'birth' and 'day' and give you a fairly accurate translation."

Tommy groaned. "You'll give us away," he said to Freddie. "Shut up about the books...we're not here to impress him! We're supposed to be thugs -- not graduates of Yale!"

Tommy's words were well said. Freddie immediately reverted to 'thug' again, but now the king's eyebrow lifted slightly at Freddie's disclosure. All was not as it should be, he thought.

"A birthday," he said, "is where you get lots of ice cream and chocolate cake and guests bring you loads of presents. But then you've never had a birthday yet, have you?"

"Naw, I ain't never had one of those. Besides, "he said with a chuckle, "If'n I did, shucks, most of my guests I probably ate, anyway!"

And with that, the King smiled. 'Maybe I just misjudged him,' he thought.

Freddie smiled. Anyone would understand a tarantula having a guest for dinner. Not to. For. Actually, Freddie had become used to eating with Brimble and Skinny Kenny. Now his appetite ran to pot pies and roasts and corned meats. In fact, if he were really to think about it, in spite of his and Tommy's posturing, how long had it been since he really had gone out at night to find dinner? He could not remember. And he liked it that way.

"Pay attention, you two!" The king was slightly put out that his newest stars were not giving this new secret weapon the full attention it deserved. "With this beautiful machine, I shall be able to have wings...to lift high over grass and bushes. I shall soar above even the green canopy of the trees. All things! Where Icarus and his father dared not dream of ...go I!"

"That's very poetic, your kingship." And here Freddie used three of his legs to gesture. Of course, being left handed as he was, they were three left hand apertures, so he lisped slightly to port as he did so. But the gesture was a big sweep in the form of a left-handed circle. Tommy said nothing; he being closer to the ground, could not spare many of his limbs for the gesture.

"Poetic, yes...but certainly not too far-fetched a flight of fancy for this foresight!" The alliteration was by accident, but all were appreciative! "If I may so myself, and I, being me, can certainly say so...myself," and he hissed a light chuckle at the absurdity of it all, "this ...THING!, as it is known, shall let me fly directly to the gold of the Leprechauns -- in daylight -- when none of the Little people, and you know who I mean by Little People! -- shall be about!" Again, he hissed a sniggle or a giggle, whichever, and continued. "This paper you see -- was drawn by Lodi during our last, shall we say, excursion, which excursion, by the way, did not end up as I wished!"

Tommy scooted across the earthen floor to slide alongside the King, who was now holding a rolled piece of paper in his tail. "Do let me see," said Tommy.

"Oh, no you shan't!" The King smiled but the look was not inviting, and rather sent chills along Tommy's backside and caused his stinger to vibrate at it's tip. "I can't trust you...I can't trust even that vile tarantula over there. This is too precious to me!" And with that, he drew the rolled map back.

"Oh, you can trust us," said Tommy, with his last two legs crossed, just for good measure.

"Perhaps I can," hissed the king. "Perhaps I can't." Then squaring himself so that his face was directly in front of Tommy, he looked into Tommy's eyes. "But then, are you afraid of heights?"

Chapter 16

Snake's Quest Continues!

Turnipseed's telephone rang -- at 9 a..m. She was just settling in for what she hoped would be a very enjoyable sleep. Next to the phone on her nightstand sat a half-full cup of now warm, not hot, chocolate. Yes, Turnipseed was one who saw the cup as half full, though today, her caller, as she would soon find out, would definitely have seen the cup as half-empty.

"Hello Lars," she said into the phone. "It is certainly not a good time to call me, for you see, I was just ready to nod off!"

There was a momentary silence on the phone. "How did you know...oh, never mind." And then again, he was silent once more while he gathered his thoughts. "You know of course, that I have sent Freddie the Tarantula and Tommy the Scorpion on a mission of great danger and intrigue...as spies to the court of the Snake King..."

"Yes, I am quite aware, Lars. What does that have to do with interrupting my morning just as I was about to get to sleep? Are they in trouble? "There was silence on the phone as Turnipseed shut her eyes, and gently touching her forehead, tried to find what was in Lair's mind. She could not make contact -- whether from too many miles separating the two, which was probably not really a factor, since at times she had been known to get thoughts from children in London or Paris or a small town in Georgia (the country, not the state) when they had lost a tooth and worried that the

tooth fairy might not be able to visit, or perhaps because her mind had basically began to shut itself down for sleep.

"No, I don't think they're in trouble. At least not yet. The trouble is that the Snake King is planning another raid to get our gold!"

"Well," Turnipseed replied with some resignation in her voice, "what is that ? Some "big deal" as the American's are wont to say? After all, he tried that once, and got so lost that he gave up and ended in the hospital. I think it's safe to say, without Lodi or someone giving him directions from the sky, that he is still not match for us. And if he were to try, what's to say that he wouldn't end up again back in the hospital?"

"I know, Turnipseed. But this time, he might succeed. He has a map that Lodi made from his last excursion..."

"Oh, really?" Now there was a glimpse of basis for the king's concern. "Do go on, your Honor!"

"Please, Turnipseed, don't be condescending to me. I know that without help from the air, he would never succeed because without seeing the creek bank and the meadow and the cornfield and the woods from high-up so that it can be seen as a total, he will never find the gold, but what makes it dangerous, is that he does have the ability now to fly!"

"Fly? You say? He, you say? Come now, Lars, how do snakes get the ability to fly? The only reason the king can do so many things, after all, is that he has been blessed with a very prehensile tail."

"A what?" Lars asked.

"A prehensile tail," Turnipseed repeated. "For heaven's sake, his tale can grasp the cup when he has tea just like your hand can. He uses his tail to write, to play cards, to brush his teeth..."

There was an awkward silence on Lars end. "Oh...I knew that."

"Certainly you did, Lars...but a prehensile tail hardly gives one the ability to fly."

"Well, he just has to put his prehensile tail into the basket below his helium balloon, and he'll still be able to fly."

"Oh! My! Fly, you say? Put his tail into a basket below a helium balloon, you say, and fly, you say?"

"Freddie and Tommy agreed to spy for us. They've become his newest guards, because no-one will believe those two are capable of being good men and true. They sent for me to meet me by the meadow last night and told me all about the king's balloon. It's a Mylar balloon that will never lose its helium, so the Snake king had a basket lashed to the bottom. He'll ride in the balloon! If the Snake's army just follows his directions from the balloon, there's a chance that they can find our gold..."

Turnipseed thought hard. "What should you worry about? Even with that fan, the wind will certainly carry the balloon away and there's no problem at all, Lars. You worry too much. It can't happen. So let me alone, that I might get some sleep! I have to get up early evening because I have a big night ahead of me tonight."

"They've thought of that, Turnipseed. They're going to tether the balloon to one of the big lizards -- an iguana -- and they'll just let the Snake King lead the way from the balloon!" Then he added ominously, "They're going to go in the next few days -- in the daytime!" He stopped to let that sink in. "Brimble and Skinny Kenny won't be there, at the pot of gold, for obvious reasons., And none of the rest of us can do anything, because we don't have daytime powers!"

'Because you've never tried, you ninny, to use your power's in the day. Just because the Leprechauns and the trolls can't, doesn't mean the faeries cannot. It's mind over faerie thoughts, my love," she thought. Then she blushed. "Thank goodness he can't read minds," she thought. 'My love? What did I mean by that?' Her breath caught, and then came in great rushes. She laughed to herself. "My love? Oh, my goodness!"

"Turnipseed? Are you there?" Lars was puzzled by the silence.

"Sorry, I just had a most insane thought," she replied, and laughed from embarrassment. "Now let's get on with this, shall we? You must remember, it's all in your mind, your majesty! There is nothing in all faerie lore that says you can't have faerie powers by day!"

"Right now I am not going to debate you. I just need your help because you can fly by day, and I can't -- no matter what the reason, I can't fly during the day!" His tone turned more serious, nearly cynical as he continued. "If the king gets his hand on that gold -- it will bankrupt all of faerieland, for we won't be able to buy or do anything that is of this modern world. No television, no radio, no phones. Nothing! We have one big person who knows about us and helps us. He never grew up, I guess. Because he can see me and frequently talks with me!"

This was an interesting sideline that Turnipseed wanted to press on, but now she began to understand why the gold was so pressing. "What do you mean, helps us?"

"Well, you must keep this secret, Turnipseed. He has run an electric line to the big sycamore tree for us, and we get our power from it. He also helps me to buy whatever we need that is new. I pay for what he buys for us, but I don't pay him anything to do it. Instead, I tell him our stories, and he writes about them in books for the Big People!" (Indeed, now you know my secret!) That's his payment."

"You say without the gold, then this Big Person can't buy us our telly's or our phone's!"

"Where do you think I get all those raspberries for you, Turnipseed? Or your favorite teas?"

"I had never thought about it, really. I just figured our little shopkeeper used his faerie power!"

"Well, a fat lot you know about that...but never-the-mind."

"Will you let me know when I'm needed?" she said.

"Of course...But can't you just read my mind?"

"Oh, how dreadful! To do that, I would have to keep you "on" as one keeps on one's radio. And frankly, as nice a gentleman as you are, I have been terribly embarrassed at the most inconvenient times by your thoughts...I mean, men's thoughts. I should much prefer that you ring me on my telly when you are ready and tell me what we should do!"

"That's the bad part, Turnipseed. We don't know what you should do!"

What I should do? Me? Last time, you came with me, Lars. We did it together. Wouldn't that be the best way? Together?"

Lars thought about the terrifying ride on Addie. He thought of looking down -- hundreds of feet down, with only the broad back of the pig and the small waist of Turnipseed to rely on for safety. And he remembered that wonderful smell of fruit. Would he be willing to risk the fear of falling with the delicious touch of having his arms about Turnipseed's waist?

"Lars? Are you still there?" And suddenly, his thoughts came tumbling through. Some weren't even in words yet, but she understood enough to feel the heat of a blush. What exciting creatures these men could be," she thought. "We're going to have to explore this a little more."

"I will call you," he stammered. And abruptly hung up. Suddenly, he wasn't thinking all about a Snake King who was going to fly in the daytime, and could find the faery gold. All he could think about for the moment, was a tiny waist and the smell of fruit.

Turnipseed drifted into sleep with a sweet feeling she had never admitted to before. All she could think about was of two strong arms wrapped tightly about her waist.

"Oh my!" was her last waking thought

Chapter 17

The Heroes awaken to a dubious task

According to Herr Professor Rosenberg's (of the University of Brammerick) monumental work of 1998, it is proven once and for all that some types of insects snore when they sleep. In the case of Freddie and Tommy, the work certainly was conclusive. The raucousness of their audio-rich tumultuous sleep was so overcoming to most other creatures that the large dormitory where they slept was now completely empty except for them. Or else sleep was an enemy for all sleepers; the other soldiers regimented to the barracks were absent now at least a fortnight -- all other's having fled into the night several nights past. After Taps, they would creep away one by one leaving only Freddie and Tommy. The two spies were not the least acknowledged of the fact, for each was so used to the fearful noise of the other that each was able to sleep in spite of the other's racket.

But their steely nerves were incredibly tuned to any other strange noise during Morpheus. As it had been when the King had entered their cave so many days hence. A light tap on their shoulder by Earnie on behalf of the king immediately brought them awake.

"Wake up you blighters!" Earnie said, holding his shield above his body in case Tommy had an involuntary reaction to being awakened.

"Who goes there," Freddie fairly shouted, somewhat stung with fear at being roused from a deep sleep.

"Keep cool! It's me -- Earnie! Wake up, you two. The king has summoned you!"

Tommy rubbed his eyes before pulling his 1912 Elgin Railroad Chronometer from his pocket and checking the time in t he presence of Earnie's lantern. "You roustabout, Earnie! I should eat you for this -- it's just four thirty in the morning -- daylight savings time!"

"I happen to know from reading that scorpions don't eat lizards such as I am, so quit your trying to get into me head over that! I said the king as sent for you -- both of you. And he wants you now! And quite your griping! I had to get up twenty minutes ago to come get you two and it's bloody dark out there, and I hate dark cause the faeries are about!"

Freddie was groping about for all his shoes, which is a major grope -- no just the finding the shoes, but deciding which ones of his rather goodly supply of limbs was for walking, and which limbs was for being arms. He paused to reply to Earnie, "Don't you worry, Earnie. I have it on good authority that faeries in any form -- from trolls to elves to fancy faeries themselves -- rather hate being close to the Snake king or his subjects here! I know that for a fact! I do."

"That would be a relief to know, but I can't believe it." He looked dourly at Freddie. "Especially coming from you."

"Bah," what would you know, "Tommy said back to him. "Let's be gone then!"

As they left the barracks, excited voices in the loudest whispers seemed to fill any gaps in quiet as the two walked along. There were creatures everywhere, but no sounds of scurrying about.

"What's all the noise, "Freddie whispered t o Earnie.

"You'll find out soon enough, I reckon," said Earnie.

Tommy leaned over to Freddie "You think they've found out about us? Do you think we're going to our hanging?"

"If we were, they would have sent far more than Earnie for us, Tommy. Let's play it out."

"That makes sense," said Tommy.

The moonlight began to reveal shapes that attached to the voices. On the other side of the courtyard they had now entered, a column of soldiers appeared, bathed in the silvered light of the half-moon. They had not noticed them until now, though the column was in place before they had entered the yard.

"What's all them about?" asked Tommy.

"You'll find out in a moment, so keep quiet lest the faeries hear you!"

"I told you, no faerie's going to be within a thousand feet! They're more afraid of you than you are of them, Earnie!" Freddie said, to emphasize his point.

The king was waiting for them in the center of the clearing, but he flitted back and forth as a madman paces in and out of a large dark shadow. Freddie looked up, so see what cloud blocked the moon. And as mountain into the midst, he saw the outline of the balloon, tethered by stakes in the clearing. Any further and the trio would have tripped over one of the lines.

The king nearly vibrated with excitement. In Italian, he was palpati, palpati! "Well, what do you think of it, me hearties!" the king questioned, not really asking their thoughts, but actually attempting to see what fear the awfulness of the moment could strike into hardened hearts.

"What are you doing with it out of the dry-dock, you majesty?" asked Freddie.

"What do you think, my spy?" And then he pulled himself up to eye-level of the monster spider, and spat, "It is time! We go at sunrise!"

Tommy glanced at Freddie and mouthed the words without sound, "We've got to let King Lars know!" Freddie understood perfectly. The Snake looked at Tommy just as he finished.

"Are you quite well, Sir Scorpion, for so shall you be at the victory of today! Your mouth moves, but no sound issues!"

"I speak alright -- I am well, your kingship!"

"Very well. Now, we shall hide here until dawn moves upon those mountains! At which time, all the little folk and their enchanted minions shall retire into the safety of their village. At that time, we shall with utmost stealth move silently into that good darkness!"

"Pithy!" said Freddie with a 'plosive 'p' on his 'pithy!"

"Very good!" exclaimed the Snake. And he hissed the word back through the most vile of smiles. "Pithy!"

Freddie and Tommy crept away as the king became involved with the details of the lift-off. They found themselves on the opposite side of the balloon, where apparently, no others had taken up stations because of the lack of light.

"We'll fail King Lars if we can't get the news about the Snake's sailing out of here in the dawn in this infernal ship!", Tommy said with some agitation. "What can we do? Even if we leave here, right now, it will be daylight before we would reach him. And by then the Snake will be quite gone!"

Freddie wrapped his cloak about his body in an attempt to stay warm. For even in summertime, it can be cool along the creek bank just before dawn. Freddie fingered his spear shaft as if he could osmosis wisdom from its' smooth wood. "Do you think that Turnipseed can hear our thoughts this far away?"

"Who knows? She could be anywhere in the world right now. Moscow -- Amsterdam, you name it. I don't know, either, how far thoughts travel."

Freddie said nothing for a moment, then he spoke dreamlike, "Is thought transfer like a radio? Does it bounce about in the air and wrap around the world? Or is it more like light -- has to be line of sight, straight on kind of thing. Or is it like a mother's connection to her soldier son who is dying on the plains of Anzio -- she immediately knows what is happening as certainly as if she were there."

Tommy looked at Freddie with almost a look of pity in his eyes. His speech decried cynicism.

"I never have thought about it at all, Tommy. I ain't so sure scorpions have much brain room for philosophy! I ain't sure we got much transmitting' power for her if she was to be standing right next to us both and we hooked our brains together to send the thought! Now get back to earth here, Freddie!"

Now even though neither of our two heroes have anything but an exoskeleton, they did have wonderful backbones! "We're all alone here, Freddie! We aren't going to get any kind of help! We just gotta do it ourselves." Tommy raised his hand in helplessness. As he looked upward by crooking his scorpion neck, he saw what you could not see in the glare of the many lights that shone upon the metallic skin. At first it appeared to be haphazard display of dark and light shadows playing along the top of the balloon, but how he could see that the balloon was rigged with a latticework of ropes -- as if crocheted! He stood staring until Freddie followed his gaze upward.

Tommy spoke, "What's that look like to you, Freddie? Huh?"

Freddie was puzzled by the question, studied the balloon intently. "Like a doily?"

"A doily! A doily? -- Freddie, you're a s-p-i-d-e-r, for heaven's sake!"

"So!"

"So?" Tommy shot back. He slid around till he was face-to-face with Freddie. He jammed two sets of hands onto his thorax. "It's a spider web. See? The ropes? They look like spider webs!"

(Haven't we all looked at something that was as plain as plain and yet we could see nothing. Then someone shows us what we see and --eureka! It jumps out at us and it is all that we see? Then we feel foolish for not having seen it ourselves until someone pointed it out to us.

"Wait a minute!" Freddie said, mesmerized as the patterns of ropes that were used to trap the balloon and tether it to gondola beneath suddenly took the form of a giant, almost magical, spider web, with spinneret's dropped down and attaching to the basket below. Then he understood why Tommy was showing him the giant web.

"Are you suggesting that just because I'm from the arachnid persuasion, that I ought to be able to crawl up there on those ropes while that..." and he paused as he sucked in his breath, "while that thing is in the air!"

"Exactly!" Tommy exclaimed. "Look at your arms and your legs...those little hooks and barbs there, big fella. Millions of years of evolution gave you those web-climbers!"

"Go on Tommy...I doubt I'm going to like what I hear, but go on."

"Well, how we going to stop his Honor, the Snake, if we don't? No Turnipseed, for she's off, giving coins to kids as the tooth faerie. And you tried to reach her, but obviously it didn't work. We're here alone. And King Lars? A great man, but he's afraid of daylight, and might I add, heights? I understand that he'll walk during the daytime rather than fly -- even if he could! " Tommy could not talk fast enough as his thoughts tumbled into words. He finally paused. "Besides," he said finishing. "I'm going with you!."

Their conversation was interrupted by Earnie. "King wants you two. Hurry! He's been looking all over for you because he's ready to launch." Earnie was flush with his new-found authority, and was a bully as all weak men are when they get authority. Usually he could only say, "halt, who goes there." but while the king prepared to launch, little Earnie was his fetch-it fetch-all. He rudely shoved spectators aside, yelling "King's man coming through! Move aside!"

The crowds split as a stream around a rock then melded back together as the group moved forward.

The event was now a party, for the kingdom had little to celebrate and the occasion of their king going aloft in an untried balloon brought nearly all the kingdomers together. There were whole families with picnic baskets in tow. Smoking torches lit up the pre-dawn and danced the crowd's movements and reflected their excitement onto the sides of the balloon.

"Where'd all these creatures come from?" asked Tommy.

"It's incredible, isn't it?" Earnie replied, still pushing through the crowds. "I know the king wasn't expecting this, so I put the word out to a few friends to pass along...and BOOM!"   He paused with great self-pleasure. "I think the king really likes it!"

They were making their way toward the king who was surrounded by a group of 15 to 20 of his subjects. The king was animated, excitedly gesturing about with his prehensile tail.

He spied the spies coming toward him and smiled his most engaging toothless grin that seemed even more gracious because of the turn-up that serpents have at the end of their jaws.

"Oh Good! Earnie found you two. I'm ready to shove off and all that. Would you care to join me in the basket?"

Tommy spoke. "If it's all right with your worshipness, we ain't much for heights, is we, Freddie.   Now, we ain't much for heights, I reckon.   We're tunnelers, diggers, creatures of the ground. Heights really petrifies me, it does...and I know it does really for Freddie too, if I might be bold as if to speak for both of us."

"He's right, your kingship!" Freddie said. Why, if you was to read about us spiders, mostly murders that we are, in the Brittanica, you'd soon know that we are creatures of sand...and dirt...and the floor of the caves and dark and dank spaces like that." He paused for effect. "We're best on the ground where we can sneak around and find unsuspecting creatures and gobble 'em up Spear 'em a few times with our jaws, or like Tommy here, jab 'em a few times with our tails for good luck."

"Britannica? Read in the Britannica? "The king squinted his eyes at the absurdity of the response. It made no sense, so he shook it off. "So you don't want to be in the balloon with me?"

"No sire. As much as we like to bask in the presence of your royalness, it appears t'us that you need someone on the ground runnin' interference for unexpected trolls or Leprechauns or the such to protect your royal presence and to keep your lizard there safe ."

Chapter 18

A Plan? What Plan?

The king was strangely dubious, but snakes aren't smart enough to hold doubts and his stern suspicion gave way to a hearty grin, one that was well-taken and well-meant. "Well said, my two evil guards. I shall reward you richly for this once the kettle of gold is safely aboard the basket!"   And with a wave of his tail, he dismissed them.

They stumbled about getting to the other side of the balloon. Their adrenalin surged -- and spiders and scorpions who are high on adrenalin stumble a lot, because they have a lot of appendages to stumble about on. Once on the other side, they saw what the bright torches had been blocking -- that cerulean blue was touched with light from the approaching dawn -- the blues were splashed above the mountains with soon the yellows and ochres to flood into the blues and the fiery fingers of white would pull the great orb, the Sun, into the new day.

Had the King looked, he would have seen two dark shapes work their way up into the rigging and disappear on the balloons far side. He might even have seen the balloon sagging so slightly from the added weight of the big spider and his scorpion companion. But at the present time, the king was far more interested in returning the adulation of his loyal subjects.

In due time, the lead rope was attached to the mid-section of the Lizard, and all was ready for the King. He slithered into the door fashioned into the basket and grabbing a white hanky by his tail, waved for all his subjects. As the handlers released the tethers and the balloon began its slow assent into the new dawn, a great roar went up from the crowed.

Earnie turned to his friend. "I don't know if they're cheering because he might fall and break his neck...I mean, body...and not come back. Or if they're all grateful for the $10 we gave each from the King's private treasury to get them to be here to see the king off! I'm glad that's one excursion we're not going on."

The "Ohs!" and "Ahs!" were heartfelt. Not just for the King, but for the genesis of flight which at last had come to the Kingdom. None of the creatures had seen flight before except for the occasional faerie at night who took a shortcut across this tiny kingdom. They watched as the balloon gently rose, wafting and bumping with every soft breath of morning breezes, floating as a boat on the currents of air.

While those below were marveling at the rising, those atop the balloon were anything but, for as the balloon rose above the meadow that day, the stomachs of the snake, his minister whom he had invited along and the two more heaven-positioned spies, sank with each inch the balloon arose.

"The last time I was this high, I fell and ended up in the hospital," the king spoke, remembering all too well his last ill-fated excursion.

The helmsman happened to be a lizard, a Sand Lizard, and as such is imperious to nearly any kind of fear, for after all, there is not much brain available to him to develop phobias.

The two on top were in absolute terror, for every time the balloon would bob, it was as if they were playing crack-the-whip with the two heroes at the end of the line -- every movement the king felt was magnified by a factor of 10 on the top of the balloon for the two stowaways. The picture certainly was not of two brave heroes, but rather of two creatures desperately holding on for their lives, certain that with every sway of the balloon, their desperate grips on the ropes would be broken and they would plunge to their deaths below. You must remember that to a spider, the tree tops are many times the spider's height, and to these two, the ground would appear as an unfathomable distance below!

Tommy grimaced and shut his eyes. In his mind, he yelled for Turnipseed to come to their rescue. "Turnipseed, Madame! Hear me out! HELP!"

Turnipseed was just that moment in the process of pulling a small tooth from under the pillow of a most beautiful young person -- perhaps it was you! It must have been you, because the smile on the child's face was beautiful as it slept.

Turnipseed had a silvery half-dollar which she was polishing on a towlett to a brilliant shine. She absently rolled the coin along the back of her fingers from one to another and finally grasped it by its edge with her thumb and forefinger, and then slipped it gently under the pillow. Leaning over, she lingered and as if with the touch of a butterfly wing, kissed the child on the forehead. The child's smile broadened for through the portals of deep slumber, where it was running free in a field of exquisite gold and pink roses (no thorns grew in the dream) and of wonderful wild daisies and lilies, the white butterfly had kissed the child's cheek.

The thought hit so suddenly it staggered Turnipseed. She involuntarily grabbed her ears as if to protect them from a loud scream. She winced as if in pain. But it was not pain, for someone -- or something-- was shouting to her in her mind. It was not such a matter of words, but of feelings. Someone was in trouble!

She tried to connect. But whoever it was, they could not receive her communication. It was only happening one way, and though the feeling of terror and helplessness lingered, the thought had been intense and short.

"I've got to get back!" she said aloud.

The child's eyes were wide open and gazing enraptured with the lady who stood in the brightness. Who stood by the bed and gently bathed the room with a soft, urethral glow.

"Tooth fairy?" the child asked. "You just kissed me away -- just like my mommy kisses me to sleep!"

Turnipseed smiled. For only a few fortunate children are every allowed to see her. "Yes, I am the tooth faerie-- and I did kiss you. And now, in the morning, you will remember, but as a dream or real, you will never know -- it will just be a sweet memory for you." And kissing the child again on the forehead, she watched as the eyelids closed and once more the child was running through the fields of flowers.

"Barty, "she thought. "Get ready. I am finished here. But someone is trying to reach me -- someone is in trouble -- terrible trouble, but I can't make out any words or thoughts. Just a feeling that someone is very much in danger! I need you to contact Lars! "

Barty was home. The work load this night had been so light, she had not needed help. Now she was glad that Barty was home, for she needed Addie's help desperately!

"Thanks for waking me, Turnipseed. I'll get right on it. But it's pretty much daylight here!"

"Daylight or no," Turnipseed replied, "We'd best act now! Somehow I feel this cannot wait -- it cannot be put off. I don't care if Lars is not comfortable in Daylight. I think he should know about this. I'll be home express!"

Lars and Barty were waiting for Turnipseed and Addie, pacing back and forth in front of his home. Turnipseed spoke first. "Careful, Lars. You'll wear a rut in the ground!"

Lars took her by her hands as he greeted her. He brushed cheeks with a kiss of greeting. He thought, "I love walnuts and apples."

Turnipseed blushed and turned her head aside with a smile. She did not want Lars to know she had tuned him in. She actually was slightly embarrassed by his next thought. "Why do men always think that way?" she mused. But she felt a quick warm glow and rather enjoyed the feeling which to her was a rare feeling indeed.

"Lars, I know you doubt your daytime flying abilities, though I have no idea why you do! There's not natural reason you not to be able to fly. But anyway, let's start cracking! We'll both fly Barty!"

Actually, Turnipseed had no intention of not riding Barty, because she loved the feeling of Lars' arms around her. And she especially liked how he had to hold on to her so tightly because of his fear.

Lars, on the other hand, even with his fear of daylight flying looked forward to the ride for the same reason. "Where else do I get a chance to be so close to such a fascinating faerie?" he thought. In fact it was hard for Lars to concentrate on the task at hand except for the enormity of the problem.

"Have you had any further contact?" he asked Turnipseed.

"No."

"I'm pretty sure it's Freddie and Tommy," Lars continued, "because they are in an extremely dangerous situation. Do you think Turnipseed, that the Snake might have bitten them?"

"Bitten them? The Snake? No, but I don't think him to be venomous anyway. Venomous creatures have no hesitancy in striking. They are rather casual about the whole thing, so all creatures fear them. As much as we dislike his rule, he is conniving, deceitful, ill-mannered and appalling transparent in his coveting our gold. But I can't classify him as evil."

"What then," Lars thought.

"What then? Why Lars, I should think that the situation is dire for Freddie and Tommy. I do not believe they are life-threatened, to be sure!" she replied, then added, almost apologetically, "Please forgive me for the thought reading."

Lars harrumphed. "How long have you been listening-in?"

Once again Turnipseed blushed, "Long enough!"

Freddie's stomach was beginning to settle down. He looked over at Tommy, who was holding on for dear life clutching at the ropes that bound the balloon. "Well, Ollie. What a fine mess you've got us in!" he said in his best Stan Laurel imitation.

"Very funny! What else could we have done? We can't get through to Turnipseed. We had no way to contact the King. So you and I were the last resort! Got any ideas? Use your great brain for this!"

The spider rested his head against two of his arms deep in spider thought! Spiders think mainly about what they're going to eat next, and I'm certain that part of their thought centers around whom they're going to scare next. But in this instance, his thought was mostly about would he survive this balloon ride and to a lesser degree how they could stop the king.

Meanwhile, in the balloon below, the snake was certain he had heard voices. He leaned over the side of the basket, holding tight to the edge with his tail. Certainly only the lizards were below, and they were so slow of wit that he was certain it was not them. In fact, most lizards were not loquacious or talkative -- especially the iguanas! They mainly just crashed about looking for vegetation to eat. (That is why the balloon moved along in jerky movements, for the iguana below could not resist a choice dandelion or pigweed. In fact, he had even found a small plot of wild strawberries which were delectable red and of course he had to stop for each and every strawberry to be eaten with relish.) And this all goes to show you why the snake was king and not a lizard. The snake might have ideas as stupid as anyone, but he forged ahead with them! He got things done!

"I hear voices," he said to his helmsman.

"I don't." was the reply.

"Perhaps it's just something on the ground then, but it didn't seem like it."

As they bob-bobbed along on each breath of air, the two spies atop sat looking over a world which seemed to be miles below them. Presently, Tommy spoke to Freddie, who now, in addition to being terrorized, was depressed and glum.

"So what's your problem?"

Freddie rolled his eyes at the obvious. "Duh! What's wrong with me? What should be wrong with me? How shall I paraphrase it so that your incredibly small, mostly reflex-driven little mind can understand it."

"Wait a minute here, bub! Just because I'm not the voracious reader you are, you don't need to make fun of me! Name calling is out of place. We've got a problem, I see you're deep in thought but don't look too happy, I make a comment about it! Bam! You're insulting me instead of spending that brain of yours -- which I might acknowledge is far greater than mine-- on something useful like getting us out a here. And also, to stop this fink king from getting the gold!" By then, Tommy was quite loud. In fact, he was screaming!

Chapter 19

Discovered by the Snake

Now the king below was quite aware of the screaming. He looked again at the helmsman, who sat with his eyes lidded over to protect them from the sun. "You idiot lizard! Don't tell me you didn't hear that screaming! "And with his fabulous prehensile tail, he pointed upwards, toward the balloon. "And it was coming from up there! And it sounded just like Tommy the Scorpion!"

The king slid up and down the entire basket, before making the announcement. "And," he bellowed, "I am going top deck to find out for myself that I am right!" And half-muttering to himself, he added, "I am always right."

Meanwhile, Addie and her two faithful companions, Turnipseed and Lars, were making a checkerboard search along the riverside, perhaps twenty feet up, looking about them for anything out of the ordinary. Had they looked up, above the tree-line, they would have seen the Mylar bag floating about just thirty feet above the tops of the tallest trees a few miles to the south. They would also have noticed with great interest just where they balloon was taking the entourage.

Freddie looked at Tommy with great surprise. "You are really caught up in this, are you not, Tommy? Bravo!" His smile showed he had no ill will of Tommy. In fact, there was a deep appreciation and affection which anyone could plainly see that existed in the spider for his scrawny friend with the stinger. "I do have a plan, Tommy. It will take your special skills -- and it will take my special skills, that is if I have any memory how to spin webs!"

Tommy was still hot under his, shall we say, thorax? "My special skills? Your web-spinning?"

"Quite correct. If you look ahead, notice what I'm noticing?" Freddie asked.

"No -- not really..." Then recognition hit him right between his compound eyes. "I dare say it, Freddie, but that looks like the Leprechauns house -- and look! The cave!"

"Precisely," the scorpion said smugly. "We have to act, because this time, that old snake is going to end up in money-heaven. " He paused, because the subject now was critical in the lives of all the little people. "But we aren't going to let him have the gold!"

"Let who do what? Are we talking about my share of the gold?" It was the Snake King, who was holding the lines with his tail and inching up toward the two.

And then at the top, he looked at the two and smiled with his evil-grin. "Afraid of heights, are we men? " With that, grabbing a line, he reared up cobra-like until he was nearly as tall as Freddie, and swaying back and forth like an upside-down pendulum, caused the balloon to careen to and fro till it was like a big children's swing. Only the ground was not right underfoot.

Both Freddie and Tommy had to hold on with all their power. At the end of one of the arcs, Tommy could nearly look straight down as if he were on the vertical side of a building. It was obvious that even acrophobia can be overcome by greed, for the Snake King now was completely unaware of the great heights he was working at.

"Isn't this lovely --" the king continued. You two -- I thought I smelt an education," he said, eyeing Freddie. "For a thug, you're pretty convincing." To Tommy, he just smiled. "So here we are, boys. You think you could stop me from finding the gold?" He turned to go down the balloon. "I'm not going to stay up here and fall off with you two." He paused, then began to sway the balloon again. "Enough 'rock and roll', kiddies -- and zoom, right over the edge you go!"

It was Tommy who spoke first this time. "You ain't gonna get to that Gold, king! We'll stop you!"

"And how are you going to do that? Come down the ropes? I doubt that...You can't let go the ropes right now, and the thought of you trying to climb down this far up like swash buckeling pirates is amusing beyond hope. My hearty laugh of the morning!"

Tommy had heard enough. With one quick jab of his tail his stinger came down quickly, with a reflex. The king turned his head, ready for the poisonous blow. But he felt no pain, and with his tail, quickly flicked all about his body. Then he looked up. Just inches away from his face, Tommy's stinger was plunged all the way into the Mylar.

"You wouldn't!" the king yelled.

"But of course, I have," Tommy said in a strange, Victor Hugo French accent. "It is in zee bag, shall we say?"

The king quickly backed down the balloon side. He just wanted the safety of the basket and then of the ground. "You'll kill us all!"

"Hardly! For Freddie and I aren't sticking around to see, right Freddie?"

"Indubitably!" Freddie said, smirking. You see, we have a little trick of nature, your royal craziness! It's called a web. I spin it into the air, then the wind catches it like a parachute. Tommy and I are going to ride this one out!" When he looked around, though, expecting some incredible response from the snake king, the King was gone.

"Where did he go?" Tommy asked.

"Who cares" was the only response he got. Then addressing only Tommy, Freddie said, "This was exactly my plan! Great minds think alike!" Pausing, he scooted around and assumed one of the world's really ridiculous poses. With his bum aimed strait-laced into the sky he strained with all his might. "If I can remember how I'm supped to make web now..."

"Tommy -- and I tread lightly here--but are you going to stand there forever with your rear stuck into that balloon? Have you thought that It might explode when you pull your stinger out?" asked Freddie, very tenuously.

"Will the Plan Work?"

"I have thought about that, Freddie. I really have! But as you know, with my pea sized brain, all I could come up with is that all that will happen is that when I pull my stinger out, all that is going to happen is that it will lose helium, and not a lot at that! The Mylar is not expandable, so it will not store energy when the rubber expands as a rubber balloon does, rather, there is a finite space inside this balloon and it has only a certain volume available, so it will just go "phtht!" and only a little of that, and by then, with your magnificent bum in the air, you shall have produced a glorious thread of filament and we shall be off! Up and away off!"

Freddie was impressed. "Only one slight difficulty there, Professor Tommystein! You forgot that as a gas, helium CAN BE COMPRESSED! AND RELEASING COMPRESSED GASES CAN BE DANGEROUS TO YOUR HEALTH!! IT'S CALLED AN EXPLOSION!"

Tommy thought a minute, but not in all capital letters as Freddie had just spoken with. In fact, his voice was quiet and subdued as he answered. "Oh -- and that too."

Chapter 20

The Plan Works! Sort of.

Down below, the king yelled at his helmsman. "We've got two hitchhikers aboard upstairs! They've got a stinger the size of your hand in the balloon! If he pulls that stinger out of the balloon, then we're in big trouble here because the balloon will pop!"

The Snake King was quite put out about the entire situation. But as always, he already was formulating a plan, albeit one thought of only by those who usually are going to be kind enough to reduce the number of available cretins in t he genetic pool. "Those imbeciles above us think we're in for a pretty exciting ride. They are not going to win, no, not by any means! Come here, helmsman," he gestured. "They think they're going to blow us up to kingdom come! Hah! Not by a long shot they're not!"

He motioned to the helmsman to kneel down, and he, the great king, slithered up the back of the lizard and reached above himself to the part of the Mylar bag that hung down and had been inserted into itself to form a belly-button in appearance on the underside of the balloon. The king began to pick at it with his wonderful prehensile tail.

"Sire -- what is the plan? Why do you stand on my shoulders? I cannot see anything!" And that was surely true, because the body of the snake was looped now around the neck and face of the helpless helmsman and he truly he could not see past it!

"Well, they have to get up pretty early in the morning to take advantage of this good king! For I shall unroll the fill tube on this balloon and let some helium out, and we shall descend gently to the ground, without any explosion as t hose two made spies above are hoping!"

Suddenly all the glory of being the king's chosen helmsman seemed to fade for the little sand lizard, and he wished that the king had not owed his family a favor!"

"Permission to abandon balloon, sire! We can get off on the tow rope, your majesty!"

The king was working with a fierce determination to free the fill-tube of the balloon and had not heard every word of the conversation but did realize it meant mutiny! "Oh Poppycock!" he yelled at the entire world. "Oh poppycock! I just about have it out!"

From above, Tommy yelled down. "Hey, you lousy excuse for a linguini, I'm gonna take it out!"

"The King yelled up at him in return, "Give it your best shot -- because I'm going to let all the helium out of the balloon and we're going to land below! Then my men will be waiting!"

Freddie and Tommy looked at each other in horror! "Pull the plug! With the helium under pressure? You know what that means?" said Freddie to Tommy.

"Yeah! Rocket time daddy!" He was ready to pull the stinger and leave the balloon behind. Now there was urgency! "Get that bum in the air and make a little silk, make a little silk!"

Freddie was straining, but no silk was in sight. He motioned to Tommy to look at Freddie's behind. "Oh, that is disgusting, "said Tommy. "Let's go! Go! GO! Let's get out 'a here! Let's amscray!"

Nothing seemed to be happening -- except there seemed to be something right at the spinnerets! Tommy looked over closely to see.

"Good heavens, man, what is that...that ...blob!" He could barely spit out the despicable word for the despicable sigh.

"It's just that. It's a blob! That's it? That's your web spinning talent -- that blob of goo?"

"Well, yes. Sort of . It is. I'm outa practice. In fact, I've never had any practice!"

"I've read that spiders can put their bums into the air and spin out a delicate web into the wind and ride the currents aloft -- across oceans and continents. And you? You blob! You make a big fat blob of goo!".

"Well, my tribe is out of practice! We're stalkers and jumpers and surprisers. We scare our prey spitless. But all this talk is not going to get us anywhere! "And he gave a big crescendo, as it were, until he was yelling at the end.

Tommy kept up his tirade. "We're going to crash and all because you ain't got any idea how to spin a web -- hidden for millions of years of evolutionary progress in that pea-sized brain of yours. Can't you find it somewhere?"

With that, Freddie stooped his front down, put his magnificent hairy backside higher into the air, and basically had another blob!

"Strain, you fool! We're going to crash!"

"I don't see you doing your part here, Tommy!"

"Whaddaya mean? I'm sitting here with my butt in the balloon! And you call that not doing my part? What else am I supposed to do? I've only got this stupid stinger stuck in the balloon!"

And that, of course, was the perfect time for the king to yell up, "Ok, you simpletons! We'll see what you think about this! I'm letting the gas out of the balloon right now!"

Chapter 21

All's well that ends -- well!

That gentle reminder from the king was all that Freddie needed! For like a large net thrown out from fisher boat, a long loop of silky webbing burst into the air, and with deft movements of its creator, it quickly formed a large parachute in the sky. Two of his arms reached swiftly out and grabbed Tommy and like one, Make the Web and the Parachute by Freddie; two, both grabbing each other to hold on for the ride; and three, Tommy released his stinger, and the parachute jerked them high and away from the balloon!

It was also at that precise moment the snake finally let go of the filling tube. The balloon was like a rocket leaping from its' tether, that upon release, jumps into the air and roars in take off. Actually, though, you and I know that when a balloon is released, the balloon acts like a disorganized idiot and zooms back and forth, up and down, to and fro and sideways a lot! All the while, the king is clinging to the basked as one who is at the end of a crack-the-whip childhood gang and flings at least a million miles an hour each time the whip changes direction! The large iguana thought that this was as perfect opportunity to catch up with more wild flowers, which were most delectable. So the ride was in ways both an adventure and opportunities. But with the weight, the rope broke, sending the large lizard crashing into a bush where he had amble opportunity, for it was a large blue berry bush.

What that meant to the king Snake was obvious, it looked like a far better ride than any could imagine, even in the best amusement parks! For the king zinged here, and zonged there, and well you get the picture, for we want to spare the king too much agony here (though heaven knows there are many who felt he deserved everything he could get and more). He even managed a perfect loopy-loop around an apple tree. He was yelling, screaming "Yahoo?! Yahoo! Hoo!" at the top of his lungs! He was hanging to anything and anyone he could manage to find within the confines of that flying picnic basket. He zoomed right by Turnipseed and Lars looking for all the world as one would surely expect him to look in this adventure. Lars merely tipped his tweed hat and said, Jolly well to the snake. They both tipped the brim of their supposed hats, though the Snake King's gesture was merely symbolic, for he dared not let go of the rigging rope that he so tightly held to.

Turnipseed turned to Lars. Her look was one of helplessness, quizzically delivered with a hint of a smile. "You don't suppose he did that on purpose, do you Lars? Is it some new kind of joyride, do you think?"

Lars did not answer, for he was transfixed with his hand halfway to his hat tip still in a salute while watching the Snake do three figure eights around three trees before the balloon rose into the air and hurled itself to the horizon and out of sight.

Freddie and Tommy had crashed mildly into some foliage of a giant elm tree, and were busy extracting themselves from their silken paragraph. Tommy took it all in, looking all about him, and with Freddie, watched the King's acrobatics and disappearance onto the horizon.

"Well, the king certainly did not head toward the gold, actually, he did go the opposite way," Freddie said, once both heroes (for they really were, you see!) were safely nestled into a crook of branches on the tree.

But Tommy was only thinking of his miraculous rescue from almost a certain death. "You saved us, Freddie! You really did! You and that beautiful butt of yours saved us! It really worked!"

"No, no! I am talking about the king. He did go the opposite way, last I could tell! He crashed over to the east -- and he should have gone to the west!"

"How would you know? We've never seen it from up here before!" As he said it, Tommy looked to the side and jumped from a transient fright. "Turnipseed! Sir King! Where did you come from? How did you know we were here?"

Indeed, there, suspended in air by them, hovered Barty with Turnipseed and Lars. Turnipseed spoke. "You called me?"

Tommy just shook his head no. "Not me..."

Chapter 22

We tie up loose ends!

"You know," Freddie spoke after clearing his throat. "I once read that scientist had no idea how a brain found in the magpie made that bird nearly as intelligent as a primate -- and yet the brain is smaller than a walnut! So, being a spider, I have no idea why, with my small brain size, which is much smaller than that even of a magpie, I still have the mental abilities of any creature! I had no idea whether my brain was big enough to put out enough thought for you to hear, Turnipseed. I actually did not think you could hear me!"

"It is the soul that thinks -- which is why the smallest of animals show fear, show anger, show kindness....it is your heart that called!" Turnipseed said, and reaching out, touched the spider with her wand. His body began to glow as magic worked its' wonders. Then she touched the scorpion, and he too began to glow. She continued, "I cannot change you from who you are, for God has created you as what you are--but yours' alone is the choice of who you shall become. You shall no longer be feared by the little people, nor will you ever have desire to do them harm, but shall be one of the enchanted. Since you saved our citizenry because of your ability to fly, both of you shall here forth have the magic to fly and be transported, day or night and you both shall live as long as you shall desire."

Who we are does truly determine how we appear to others, for kindness cannot be hidden, nor is it ever other than beautiful to look upon. And indeed, from that time forth, Freddie and Tommy became true favorites of all the little people and their children, and divided their time between the Leprechaun's home and the village of the little people.

As for the Snake king? Well, Lars and Turnipseed did pay another visit to the hospital, and glad to say, both the king and his helmsman seemed to be the better for all their travails.

As for the iguana, we understand he got a bellyful of sweet wild strawberries that day, and is still known to disappear for a week or so every spring when the winds are warm and fruit-scented from the ripening fruit, although he has never shared his secret of the strawberry's location with any other creature in the Snake's kingdom. In fact, he has been known to tell the others that he believes the strawberries are his reward for the embarrassment he had to endure with the king that day.

And they all lived to have another adventure another day.

The end

Made in the USA
Charleston, SC
27 March 2016